WILL MOUNTAIN COX is a writer from Portland, Oregon, living in Paris, France. His work has appeared in *Forever Magazine, Hobart, Vol. 1 Brooklyn, Shabby Doll House*, and *The Drunken Canal*. He is the author of *With Paris in Mind* and was a cofounder of the literary magazine *Belleville Park Pages*. He is a graduate of Boston University and Sciences Po. This is his debut novel.

By the same author
With Paris in Mind

ROUNDABOUT

by
Will Mountain Cox

Roundabout

A NOVEL

Will Mountain Cox

RELEGATION

Relegation Books, USA

First Edition

Copyright © 2023 by Will Mountain Cox

An earlier version of *Pierre and Sarah, as if they'd never left*,
first appeared in *Vol. 1 Brooklyn*.

Designed by Zach Dodson
Author Photo by Séverine Stahly

Printed in the United States of America

ISBN: 979-8-9867670-1-7
Library of Congress Control Number: 2023935470

Relegation Books, LLC
Falls Church, Virginia
www.relegationbooks.com

For Lauren Cerand
and Giancarlo DiTrapano

and always for ï

"In short, spaces have multiplied, been broken down and have diversified. There are spaces today of every size and every sort, for every use and every function. To live is to pass from one space to another, while doing your very best not to bump yourself."

—Georges Perec, "Species of Spaces"

Rachel's back, tanned and burning
Matt feels good and can't say why
Jude and Léa have a happy baby
Marie feels bad but can't say how
Eli repeats his favorite story
Matt and Marie get back together
Pierre and Sarah, as if they'd never left

*We went to a lot of parties in January. And then again in
November. Parties were, we guessed, what you'd call them. The
parties always started and then grew, sadder, bigger, red-wine
drunk, the drunk made sadder by the long strings of Christmas
lights strung for ambiance in the badly decorated apartments.
By the entries was always a line of all-white Adidas shoes, the
ones everyone was wearing at the time. As more people arrived,
the line of shoes would grow like all-white rabbits multiplying.
No one we knew had ever seen rabbits multiply but we'd all seen
videos of the shootings. Actual humans doing the opposite of
multiplication. At the parties, the videos of the shootings would
play on the televisions, muted, while George Brassens music
played from the speakers. Everyone at those parties told stories
about how close they'd been. How they got shut in just down the
road, behind flimsy metal screens. How they'd heard the noises.
The shots. Everyone we knew was so close to the shots. And
everyone we knew loved to say so. Everyone we knew made sure
we knew it. At one of those parties was the girl who'd been there.
The one with a hole in her shoulder. The one with the best friend.
We all knew her. She didn't have to say where she'd been because
we knew already. That party had started and gone immediately
silent. That party was a bad party, really. No one was talking.
Because that girl was there. And her best friend was dead. And so
she had the better story.*

Rachel's back, tanned and burning

The eight of them sat around a circle table, themselves taking on a circular shape, an imperfect ring hugging an unchanging guide—their table, in their bar—the geometry not far off from the old roundabout circling around outside the dirty plate glass windows. Inside the roundabout grew a dry beech tree three stories high. Inside the bar sat Rachel, Matthew, Jude and Léa, Marie, Eli, and then the empty chairs of Pierre and Sarah, their absence so fresh it was itself still embodied. And outside the roundabout, Rue des Cascades and Rue Levert, Rue de la Mare and Rue des Envierges, Rue des Couronnes and last, la Mare's other arm. Six concrete paths converging to form a traffic circle high up on the hills east of Paris.

It was late but still light thanks to the long Parisian summer with its blued-out evening silvers. Inside the bar it was dark, with the bar lights cutting on and off intermittently, a kind of twinkling to replace the night sky's missing stars, a side effect of being connected by old extension cords that crisscrossed coat hooks bored into the ceiling. Their bar was a bric-a-brac bar, like so many bars in Paris used to be, with useless, hoarded trinkets lining the walls, a unique patron, and a broken toilet. At this particular bar, the hoarding of choice concerned giraffe statues, of which there must have been hundreds, but a collection about which the bar's owner, Karim, would never speak nor seem to play any part in growing. Giraffes appeared, more every day, and Karim looked the other way. Instead, Karim was more often concerned with boasting about his bar's storied history as a place for hiding, having apparently hidden Communards, Resistance moles, and other lesser-known revolutionaries. Now it hid these eight, who'd seen Karim open no fewer than three doors in the bar's floor and walls that they had not been aware of before Karim first stepped through them.

Jude and Pierre had been the first to find the bar, years ago, when they'd briefly lived together after university in the converted garage at the top of Belleville Park. The apartment was cold, sickeningly so, with a concrete floor laid over by unaffixed linoleum. They laughed at the shoddy front door made of corrugated iron giving onto a side alley clearly better attuned to the selling of drugs than to the living of life. But cold as it was, the toilet window hung over the bluff of the park like a sagging earlobe and the park overhung the flat expanse of the city like the most gorgeous dislocated shoulder, giving the toilet a clear view from left to right of the Pantheon, Notre Dame, Montparnasse, Pompidou, Tour Saint-Jacques, and, of course, the Eiffel. So Pierre and Jude took the apartment. And when the city was at its coldest, with a winter film of crystallized pollution hanging fuzzy over the capital as its fog, Jude and Pierre would stand together in the toilet, in agreement that their view was the most beautiful in the whole of Paris.

The bar was a short walk from the apartment, down Rue des Envierges, and when Jude and Pierre passed it the first time, Jude peered through the windows and said it looked terrible. They went in. They called Eli, who found the bar an easy walk from his mother's, up Rue des Couronnes. Quickly they were joined by Rachel and Marie, who came down Rue de la Mare from the Métro and said it hadn't taken any time to get there, coming up the line eleven. *No time at all*, they said. And when they got the bill that first night they looked down at it, then up at Karim like he was either an angel or an imbecile, both maybe, but they didn't argue. They all came back the next night, found the bar pleasantly empty and the price of the beers uncorrected. A month later, after meeting Léa in a lecture, Rachel brought her to the bar. Léa came from down the stairs on Rue Levert, her apartment conveniently just up in Télégraph. Her coming caught Jude off guard. Two months later, when Matthew moved to Paris, he took an apartment on Rue des Cascades to be close to Jude, the only person he knew in the city. The second he'd soon know would be Marie. And when Pierre brought Sarah to the bar on their first date, a day after he'd brought another girl to the bar on a different first date, Karim told Sarah it was nice to see her again, which confused Sarah and caused Karim, who quickly realized what he'd done, to always treat her very nicely. The bar on the roundabout was theirs for no better reasons than it was cheap and they each flowed easily toward it, turned easily in it. There were usually few other customers competing for space, except on the rare occasions when something shifted slightly in the Paris atmosphere and the bar became terribly crowded.

In such cases, Karim made sure these eight were the first to be taken care of.

But on normal nights it was only these eight, give or take a lonely old drinker, and there was room in the bar to stand and turn and laugh and cry and argue and dance and throw oneself, for whatever reason, into the arms of any number of best friends to one's right or left and thus begin turning together, or better yet, turning all at once.

On this particular evening Rachel sat, red and shifting, uncomfortable in a sunburn that was failing to turn. She was responsible, at least partially, for her pain. She was both sad and furious while the circle went on talking, turning. Always talking and turning. Always going on. Peugeots and Renaults and Citroëns went turning through the roundabout outside, their headlights beaming through the bar windows, stage-lighting their faces at haunting, unflattering angles.

But what did he say this time, Rachel, specifically?

Il est con.

Non, c'est un connard.

Who cares what he actually said. He's a piece of shit.

Mais, let her speak.

Rachel, what did he say?

The Paris night was full of the dull heat that came annually with a return to responsibility. Rachel could remember this weekend jammed up inside every year of her life. Twenty-five iterations of the same pre-*rentrée* weekend, the two days buffering good summer from hectic autumn. Rachel hated this weekend for the confusing energy it gave her friends, friends who changed or had been replaced throughout her life, but whose energy, on this particular weekend, was reliably consistent: expectant energy, solution energy, energy for arguing. Three days before, Rachel had been calm and alone, perched on a rocky outcropping in the Calanques outside Marseille, frustratingly pale but excited to go home, excited to see Maxime after their long week apart. Excited for Maxime to see her body perfectly browned. In the sun, she had felt herself getting hotter and hotter. Now, Rachel ran clammy fingers across her tender clavicle.

He said it was because of the job offer.

Comment ça?

What about the job offer?

The job in general.

Il est con.

Connard.

Bâtard.

Salopard.

What the fuck does that even mean?

Male prostitute.

Male slut.

No, what does he mean, *the job in general?*

Matt had been thinking for weeks that the job would be a bad fit for Rachel. But he wasn't about to say that out loud. The long hours, the pressure. Matt looked down, continuing across Rachel's chest, still small, still perfectly shaped, but bubbling under the shame of the burn. He could imagine the sides of the bathing suit she'd been wearing pressing into her ribs, making divots. He could imagine the straps of the bathing suit having been pushed down, hanging lazy by her side. Then Matt thought of her suit bottoms and he grimaced. Matthew actually liked Maxime, though he'd never respected him. Now Matt respected Maxime even less for what he was giving up. Rachel was like Matt's sister. With years of training, he'd convinced himself he saw her that way. Matt knew he should feel angry, protective. He told himself not to feel happy. He told himself not to stare at her chest the way he was starting to, again. Like he had when he'd first moved to Paris and Rachel had taken him places that she, a real Parisian, had thought important for him to see, empty places at the edges of the city, where they would sit and Rachel would talk to Matt about men not dissimilar to Maxime. Instead, Matt looked up, saw Marie watching him, and tried to move past it, out the windows, out to the roundabout with its single tree, the tree's leaves crunchy and starting to fall. Two boys leaned against the tree, smoking and ashing dangerously into the leaves.

It's because he's jealous. It's always the same with Maxime.

C'est pas ça.

No, that *is* it. That has always been *it*.

No it isn't. It's because I've been so...

I swear to God, if you finish that sentence I will murder. You first, and then him.

Jude loved when Léa got angry, but it worried him. Léa wasn't drinking, so Jude wasn't drinking either, and that meant the anger coming off Léa was total. He thought the anger probably wasn't healthy for either of them. Or worth it. But still, the anger made the angles of Léa's face that much stronger and the passion added a certain raspy treble to her voice. Maxime was such a weak catalyst for conversation, like so many new boys had been for certain members of the table. Fodder for gossip, animus through which the group could release its aggression, dolls they could rip limb from limb. Ultimately, Maxime was hot and he could make people laugh. Maybe the hottest and most funny boy Rachel had yet presented them. But he wasn't anything more interesting than that. He was worthwhile for Jude, however, in the knock-on way Rachel's romantic happiness had a direct influence on Léa's happiness generally. Jude knew that Léa wanted to see herself mirrored in Rachel. That Léa not so secretly hoped Rachel would settle quickly, then come along with her. Jude thought back to his first days in the city, getting to know the both of them. Trying to decide who was smarter. Léa. And who was better looking. Léa. And then Jude thought about how, two weeks earlier, on a night when Léa had stayed home, a drunk Rachel had rested her head on Jude's shoulder and asked if Jude could help get Léa off her back.

Léa put her hand on Jude's back and let the violence of her frustration massage him instead. Maxime was a person who deformed the circle, by way of Rachel, changing its symmetry with the selfishness of his whims. With the susceptibility of his idiotic resolutions. Once, Maxime had explained to Léa how he was working on lucid dreaming in order to better research his thesis on Jung. Léa knew this ultimately amounted to Maxime demanding that Rachel sleep on the floor—of her own apartment—for weeks at a time. A demand Rachel agreed to, seemingly without protest. It didn't satisfy Léa to learn through Rachel what Maxime was compensating for. Léa had told Jude and Jude had said he knew that the moment he met Maxime. But nonetheless, Maxime had the power to make Rachel a weak person Léa hated and Léa hated Maxime for that most of all. For the fragility he injected into her life. For the ugliness he'd brought upon the gorgeous summer they'd all just passed through: Léa's last real summer. And Léa wanted a drink. A fuh-king *drink*. Léa turned to watch the bar, with Karim behind it, like always, washing glasses by hand, squat and palmy hands, with his thick, Mediterranean fingers, setting the glasses to drip-dry on the bar, the glasses and Karim's hands slowly dripping beads of water down their sides like the beads of sweat running down Léa's aching back.

He said he's been thinking about it for a long time.

It's only been three months since the last time.

That was different.

No it wasn't different. *Pas du tout, Rachel*.

Marie thought back to three months ago, how beautiful Rachel had looked while she cried, how nice she'd felt to hold on to. Marie remembered the odd sort of sympathy she felt, tired sympathy, at seeing her oldest friend break apart again, and how Rachel's emotion didn't fit the season, the June. The heat of the night was more fitted to jealousy and Marie had been proud of herself not to have felt any. Rachel was one of the lucky few who got to experience the pains of surplus. She was allowed to sit in rooms, teary-eyed in balmy springs, thinking that, for everyone, failures made for greater opportunities. That breakups only predated gettings back together. Or better, gettings with better-looking replacements. Rachel was the sort of person who could take off her jeans with others watching, put on sweatpants, and find true relief. Marie hadn't felt frustrated then because, at the time, at the start to the summer, she was herself finally content. She had been able to coo and stroke and say, *Everything will be alright*, and believe she was speaking the truth. But now that Marie's summer was being bookended by someone else's pain, a summer that had been filled by and dedicated secretly to overcoming her own, to bolstering her own defenses, Marie was now silently fuming. Rachel's pain was nothing more than a kink in the predestined crises of life. Marie breathed sickly air into her hot lungs and thought about how no one at her office was good-looking; not any of them, the men or the women, the managers or the interns, and how even as ugly as they were, none of them ever seemed to pay her any extracurricular attention anyway.

He's allowed to feel how he feels, but he's not allowed to be cruel about it.

C'est ça le problème. La cruauté.

I'm sick of people not being able to make up their mind. People need to stop fucking around, pretending they don't know what they want.

At least he won't be in Paris to figure it out.

Tu sais où il va aller?

Non.

Do you know how long he will be away for?

I don't know.

Maxime owed Eli money. Eli thought of the money and tried to remember what Maxime had said it was for. Something related to Rachel. Something related to a gift. But Eli hadn't heard of Rachel receiving anything. And Eli knew Maxime didn't work enough to afford travel. So, if somehow Maxime had taken a trip out of town, like Rachel said he had, Eli understood how he'd most likely gotten there. Eli had always known Maxime would turn out to be the type of boy who teetered between being absolutely loved and totally reviled. Once, alone with Maxime in the asphyxiating smoking room of some dirty club, Eli had said to him, *You're not long for our world*, to which Maxime winked and shrugged his lips, sort of like blowing Eli a kiss. Eli thought again about the money. He had always felt powerful in his generosity and tried not to worry over what it funded or what it damaged. He had unearned resources. He gave away his cigarettes and invested in intoxicants and then he doled out purposefully bad advice. Eli lavished others for a reason: to fund risk, to promote love and wilder stories. Rachel was a person—a smart and pretty, if fragile person—and she would have to feel the pain of her self-inflicted risk just like Eli and the rest of the circle had to, no matter how much better-looking or less equipped she was to handle it. But he did worry that maybe he had done something *bad*. Or at least contributed to it. And he especially didn't like wondering if he had done something to make the group less *good*, and that he would not at least partially be paid back in some unquantifiable measurement of fun now that Maxime, who was constantly fun, would no longer be around. Then Eli thought of Rachel dancing, how she was always the one in their dance circle who made the group really go. Especially when it was hot and she would lose the limits of her corners, mouth corners and elbow corners going all over the place, making Eli feel looser and more forgetful. Eli thought back to how they had danced together in hot, high *chambre de bonne* apartments in high school, apartments of their friends' hot older brothers, and how Rachel had showed Eli how to swing his arms in distraction, distractions in order to steal said brothers' most prized little trinkets, no matter how worthless they might be. For the fun of it. For the rush. Eli was frustrated knowing they wouldn't dance that evening, with Rachel feeling how she did. Or if they did dance, Rachel would probably go home before they went, like she did when she was sad, and going dancing wouldn't be as worth it. Eli looked across the table at Rachel and tried to mime begging with his eyes.

He's going to be back in a couple months saying he was stupid and confused, or whatever he always says.

You can't take him back again.

Just drop it. Really. Let her live.

Fine. How was Marseille? You got some color.

That's an understatement.

Mais meuf, tu as vachement brûlé.

My *petite crème brûlée.*

Shut up, Jude.

Have you been using cream? It looks awful.

Pierre and Sarah sat naked and sweating on their new back patio, looking at the photo of Rachel's burn that Léa had sent to the group so Pierre and Sarah could see. They felt pity for Rachel. They alone understood why she had such a bad burn. And so it was their burden to help bear, both the shame in having designed a failed plan, and equally the skin cancer. They were only forty minutes away by train. They could go and console Rachel. But the thought of forty minutes felt like weeks in the heat. Sarah and Pierre looked at one another and knew without speaking that they would not be going. At almost the same moment, the couple thought of their own romance, namely the shame in its beginning. Pierre remembered how he'd purposefully reserved himself when he'd first met Sarah, when Sarah so clearly liked him. He remembered making himself feel apathetic in her presence, all while dreaming of candid romantic acts to win her, but to win with a guise of spontaneity. There were the nights Pierre went to visit Rachel, late, after his evenings spent with Sarah, to ask Rachel's advice on molding the situation, making it bend before him. Rachel's advice had been so savagely cunning. He remembered saying, *Really?* and Rachel saying, *Trust me*, and then Rachel looking out her window into the *cour* of her building like she could see in through all the rear windows of femininity. The image of Rachel on those nights lingered like a statue in his mind, and a statue on her bed, her bare legs tucked up and her body reclining, an odalisque in marble. And when Pierre asked Rachel a second time if she was sure, she responded, *I'm only telling you this because I owe you, for I am like Cupid reviving Psyche, and you, Pierre, are the golden ass.* And then she laughed. Pierre hated the memories, the thought of how his apathy, and Rachel's advice, had almost convinced him his desires were childish, false, French; that he didn't even like Sarah. The memories of Pierre's youth scared him. But not nearly as much as how well Rachel's advice had worked. *Crispy*, Pierre wrote in response to the photo.

Well done, Sarah wrote. She set down her phone and put her hand on Pierre's thigh, immediately feeling the thin layer of sweat between them. Sarah remembered how powerful her feelings for Pierre had been at first, how she would have burned anything up or down to be with him. And then she remembered the shame that intensity had made her feel. And then, how she'd purposefully reserved herself in response after asking Rachel out for a coffee in hopes of getting Rachel's advice on Pierre, which Rachel had so freely given and Sarah had so attentively followed, even though at that time, the two hardly knew each other. Sarah remembered the torture she'd felt turning so cold toward Pierre, and the two weeks when she didn't hear from him at all. How she'd asked Rachel out a second time, to a bar on the Canal, and Rachel had nearly laughed in her face until she saw how much Sarah was suffering, at which Rachel grabbed Sarah behind both her knees, spun her so they were face to face, leaned in close, Rachel's lips wine-stained and quivering, and nearly shouted, *Get a grip Sarah, it's just a boy*. And just like that, Sarah remembered the ridiculous acts of romance Pierre began performing. She felt shame for inciting them, but loved herself for having got the calculus right. They got there, Sarah and Pierre, though it took nearly two years together for their powers to balance, for their feelings to privately equalize, for them to trust one another. And so now they no longer asked Rachel for advice. Pierre and Sarah exhaled together. Then they looked to the blisters on Rachel's body and felt pity, because they had one another, and they were sure.

And pity was exactly how Rachel imagined Pierre and Sarah would have felt had they been there. Had they not basically quit Paris two months prior. Had they not left her alone with the most difficult among them. Pierre's, a more motherly pity, one of having been there and done that, in hindsight. Sarah's, a nice fatherly pity, with an anger that didn't proceed violence or embarrassing consequences. Rachel missed the two of them. She wanted their pity, their stand-in parenting. She wanted to curl up in their sureness and have them approve of her. Rachel remembered Pierre as a teenager, so precocious with emotions, so prodigious in emotional solutions. She could feel the power he gave her when, sitting inside her locked bedroom, years ago, he'd asked, *Does this have anything to do with your parents? I know they act happy in public, but I've been wondering…*and

29

Rachel remembered crying and asking Pierre how he knew, because no one had ever noticed before. He didn't answer the question, he just told her she deserved better, that she had the potential to become someone special, and that she should cut herself off from them as soon as possible. If she didn't, she risked becoming them. She used to wonder what had happened to that Pierre, the Pierre who knew. Then, months later, she remembered Sarah saying to her, *Pierre told me about all the stuff with your parents. He told me not to tell anyone, but I just want you to know I understand and I hate it. And if you need a place to stay, or to get away, I'll help. I owe you. I have money.* Rachel had told her then, so many years ago now, that everything would be alright. And it was. Rachel watched the window, out it and into its reflection, the circle's traffic building up and relieving, changing and reordering, ordering more drinks and honking and always continuing to turn. She told herself to pay attention to her friends and not the window and definitely not to think of Maxime. A minute later, she told herself not to think about him again. A minute later she decided that thinking about Maxime was better than thinking about so many other things.

Outside, the spotlights of the Eiffel wove round through the low-hanging clouds while a wedding's carcade of German autos entered the roundabout and began to spin through it. BMWs, Mercedes, and Audis, the husband Kabylian, the wife Kabylian, both hanging out windows, the cars honking leftward and the asphalt friction fighting the cars right, tires screeching, the drivers and the riders shouting into the air while a whole playlist of different songs played simultaneously. Some of the drinkers and smokers on bar terraces stood and began clapping and dancing, while those from the wedding party whose cars couldn't fit in the roundabout parked, got out, and began dancing too, men and women pinching at the equal rations of pain in their foreheads, throwing the pain up into the sky, where the spotlights swept the pain away. Tongues in smiling mouths trilled joy like boiling water, the old beech tree breezing in the commotion and, caught up and bumping in between the dancers' living hips, the ghosts of at least three Communards, awoken, confused but happy, dancing in a shimmering, heat-wave way. Then, as fast as the party started, it ended, the cars proceeding out down Rue des Cascades. To the north, in Belleville, some of the apartment lights turned on, glaring. And to the south, in Ménilmontant, some lights turned on and were then immediately turned off again.

In the spring, the Seine promptly flooded its promenades with water. Yellow was the water, and murky too. It matched the spring sky of election season and some of us spoke in documentary voices. One evening we crossed the river on our way to an election party. From the bridge we looked down in. There were no answers in the river. It was just pretty in its drawn-out, yellow-tough question. At the party, Brassens was playing. His music was starting to mean something new. The party had no television, but it had a view onto a tall new-build building with rows and rows of windows. We listened to the election on the radio, pausing Brassens to listen, some of us watching the living rooms of the building we could see into. There were dozens of living rooms, each with their own television making colors. When the results burst in we watched the living rooms begin churning. Hands were thrown toward the sky, toward God we guessed. And remote controls were thrown screenward, useless. The apartments with nice decorations looked angry. So too the apartments with no decor at all. Someone said that was interesting. Someone said they couldn't understand. We all knew we were not sure. It seemed like everyone we knew wanted the coverage turned off quickly and the Brassens to be turned back on. Only later did our waiter friends who worked at experimental restaurants say they'd seen anyone remotely happy. They assured us though, the people who were happy were really very happy. They made up for the rest of us.

Matt feels good and can't say why

Filling out the roundabout were never fewer than three bohemians, the sort who were beautiful in the Paris of the 1990s, meaning they wore leather jackets and boots, loved rock music and mussed hair, and now had at least one but never more than two missing teeth. They shared the space with children who tided through the circle, constantly pulsing, in exchange with balls that moved in similar directions, often of their own accord due to the roundabout's slight southwesterly slope downward toward Rue des Couronnes and Rue de la Mare. Around the roundabout there was a tabac that claimed a fat, low dog whose belly dragged, who the tabac clients called Cigarillo, though that was not his name. There was also a bakery, a school, a laundromat, and two other bars, one billing itself for artists—the source of the bohemians, who leaked from it—and the second a bar-restaurant for the gentrifiers, where wine was somehow cheaper than at the bar for artists, a truth that confounded the neighborhood. The bar-restaurant served good food but bad french fries. The artist bar, bad food and no french fries at all. On this evening, a man stood in the raised dirt heart of the roundabout, the heart held in a ring by a circle of old paving stones. At first, the man seemed to converse with the beech tree, nodding to it, looking it up and down. The conversation was civil until it appeared that the tree began teasing the man, then downright insulting him. Insulted, the man began circling the tree, taunting it, saying something the likes of, *Move why don't you.* Unflinching, the tree stood firmly planted. So as not to lose face, the man promptly began fighting the tree, but slowly, like a Brazilian dancer fights, with spins and kicks and dangerous flashings of his own ass. In the dark, few saw the man, but those who did thought to themselves, *What the hell is going on.* The man was drunk, clearly, but that didn't seem to have anything to do with it.

I'm an animal and this is it, or rather, that's how Matt had looked, could be described as looking, as Rachel caught his expression behind her, over her shoulder, in the reflection of the bar's glass door as she pushed it open and entered. Rachel shivered. It was an autumn night but it felt more like winter and Rachel's sweat from the circle's recent dancing was still beaded along her neck. Matt had looked happy for the first time *in ages,* as he would have said. At the club beside the canal's water he'd moved his body in graceful angles, pumped his fists in imperfect rhythms, made noises like a wild pig. And when the rest of them had wanted to quit, Matt had demanded more. More. More. More, with a pleasant desperation. So instead of going home alone or in their stale pairs to take off their jackets and pants, the circle had instead acquiesced, specifically Rachel, who for reasons she could not explain was feeling drawn to *Matthieu*, as she called Matt when he was being wild. Sometimes, recently, Rachel had wished she felt different about Matt because that would make everything so much easier. But Rachel knew that would never work for Marie. Regardless, here they were, at the bar, like always. Rachel felt happy, too; happy by diffusion, happy by surprise. She'd danced hard and harder. Her body had become tired in a good way. The old way. And for a long second Rachel found herself caught in the slow-motion silence of fleeting happiness, with Karim filling beer glasses and wine glasses, the circle flexing through the bar's strangers, and their collective muscular relief of their settling in. A muted rain began to pelt the glass of the windows and grease the traffic circle. Rachel remembered Matt as he'd been before, *Matthieu,* long before it felt like now, and how he seemed to be again. Rachel watched as Matt bought a round of beers, slapped Jude on the back, and began to sing along with the music. She shivered a second time, this time at the thought of time's speed returning to normal.

Bienvenue à Paris.

What?

Welcome to Paris.

We live here.

Ah oui? But you don't speak French.

Je parle français.

Et alors, pourquoi tu cries comme une pute?

Matt had been speaking loudly. He felt good. There'd been an unnamable flexing in his abdomen all night that had made him want to scream. So now, if he was, all the better. The boy speaking to him was someone he'd never seen. Someone who'd definitely never been in their bar before or else Matt would have noticed. The boy stood beside Rachel and started talking to the circle but kept looking down at Rachel's body and smiling. The two peaks of his lips made dangerous angles. Matt smiled and laughed to convey disbelief at the criticism and then felt his abs getting tighter. Behind the boy was another group, all male, a smaller circle all with their jackets removed but with their scarves still on. Matt laughed again. The boy noticed. For Matt, the night had been perfect. The circle had eaten Chinese at the good place on Rue Jules Romains where they let you bring your own wine. At points through the meal Rachel, Jude, Léa, Marie, and Eli each had grease running down their chin. That had made him laugh. Then they'd gone dancing at the café on Boulevard de la Villette, the one that was always wet inside with condensation, the one where prostitutes still milled about outside looking for work, the sort of place that made Matt feel very European. Dancing inside the café the group had become singular, spinning and leaning, trying rockabilly moves none of them knew how to do correctly. That had made him smile. Now they were at their bar up in one of the last hills of the city, as if they were remaking their own Montmartre, continuing the night, everyone close to home so no one could feel guilty about staying out. Nothing was different from what the circle did normally except for the feeling in Matt's abdomen. Matt was worried about losing the feeling. He was terrified because he loved the feeling and hadn't felt it, really felt it, in so long.

We're having a good time so how about you fuck off?

Doucement. Is this guy your boyfriend?

Arrêtez. S'il vous plaît.

Ah une vraie française. Bon. You could really do better, I think.

And you could get fucking battered, *mec.*

The boy put his arm around Rachel's shoulders. She tried to pull away but he held her.

What's up with your friend? He seems a bit unstable, *non?*

The fuck did you just say? Stop fucking touching her.

Sarah felt a chill run through her looking out her kitchen window at her yard and the way its single tree bent in the bad weather. Trees felt different outside the city, like they could crack at any moment and fall without warning. Sarah loved her yard in the daylight, the green of it, with all its potential, but at night the yard became a terrible movie. It morphed and its edges grew hiding places not filled with her friends. In so much empty space, Sarah could imagine too many horrors. Too many men wrapped up in masks, wanting something of her. She knew Pierre was just in the next room over, taking advantage of all the space they had agreed they craved. She could easily go find him and ask him for comfort but Sarah didn't want to seem weak. She didn't want him to think she was having regrets about their new life, even though now, after nine months, it wasn't so new. Sarah knew how important it was for Pierre to be away from Paris, to focus on his work, even though Sarah was sure their friends resented her for taking Pierre away, thinking the exodus was her idea. The thoughts hurt Sarah because they reminded her that ultimately the friends were Pierre's, even if they'd become like a family to her, sisters and brothers she'd never had. Sarah thought about yelling to Pierre, *Everything alright over there?* but realized it wasn't Pierre she'd be asking. She'd be asking the night, with her friends in it, somewhere else.

Pierre was in the bedroom looking at his phone, at the ticking clock on its lock screen. He felt a chill, shivered, and attributed it to distance and to his intuitions. It was only a ten-minute walk to the station and a forty-minute train ride to the city. Pierre could feel that there was a problem, back in Paris, that would soon need solving. Pierre knew if he and Sarah left now, they could make it for a last drink. Maybe two even. Plenty of time for solutions. But Pierre's house was warm and perfect. In it, he could extend his arms. In it, he had his own second room, to work. And in it he worked well. The wood boards of the floor were clean and the bathrooms were without mold and the smell of the home was only of candles and their bodies, not anybody else's. There was no reason to leave. Outside they would get wet and cold. And if they did go, they would have to stay the night at Jude's and Léa's, taking up what little deficit space their friends had until the morning, until the trains started running again. Conversely, in the house, Pierre never felt needed. Needed like all his friends used to need him and come to him first, with their need. Like when Eli's dad passed and, though Eli was closer to Rachel and Marie, Eli came to Pierre asking how to best protect his mother. Or like when Léa was convinced that Jude was planning to move home and she came to Pierre with hopes that he would know how to stop him. Those were the sort of needs he missed, that seemed to disappear once his friends had to take regional trains to see him. And in the missing need, Pierre felt the chill turn to danger. He knew something bad was about to happen. *Everything alright over there?* he called out to Sarah. Pierre heard Sarah laugh in response, but he didn't understand why. He checked his phone again. The 23:52 train would just be leaving, heading straight for their bar and the problems in it.

I don't think you want to hear what I've got to say, *frère*.

Go on then. Give it a go. Or maybe you could take your scarf and get fucked.

Your boyfriend isn't a very smart boy.

Léa backed away from the circle, out of an instinct she'd never felt before, one she'd told her friends society had made up, one she told her friends didn't exist. Matt was smiling, so it would have made more sense to move closer to him, to latch on to some of his happiness. She'd stood near him all night and noticed Jude standing near to him too, on Matt's other side. The realization made her smile, the fact that subconsciously they were practicing a new form of collective protection they were learning without knowing it. She'd wanted to stoke Matt's positivity, to instill it on him for the future, since Matt was basically now her family. And she felt proud to know that Jude was capable of doing the same, looking out, being conscious of their new need to make everything around them the safest and best possible. Léa thought for a moment about Jude's stories of his youth, growing up with Matt, and what Matt was like as a child. She wondered what it was that turned boys into men and men into babies. What made happy children into depressed adults, and vice versa. Léa wondered what it was that gave people so many drastically different personalities during one little life. Who was responsible for such tragedies? Léa wondered if it was her. If it could be. Léa tried to remember what it was that was so odd about Matt's mother and couldn't. But now, she remembered, there was something more to her, to her and Jude, that was bigger than Matt. Foundationally more important than making sure Matt felt good, regardless of his decisions. Safety. So she backed away and planned a quick path to the door, if she needed it. She looked at Jude, wanting her eyes to prompt him into action, into doing something. Léa saw Jude looking back at her and she saw that he already was.

Jude felt a calling, like he'd always felt war would feel. Not the new wars they had now. Old war, war-song war, with its dreams of peace. Jude remembered playing imitation war games with Matt, at school, with their little bodies that would shout their way into achieving seriousness and imitating men. He remembered how the games would usually transition from the heroic charges and forced retreats into the weekly beatings Matt would bait his way into receiving from the older boys, bigger than him and better at war. Jude could still feel the confusion when, in his attempts at rescuing Matt from his beatings, sometimes Matt would set upon Jude himself, Matt lost in a punch-drunk tantrum, the two in their dirty little uniforms, Matt punching and punching Jude, and the bullies laughing at the spectacle. Jude had learned he had to wait out the fights safely from the side, watching Matt's frail little body, with kid-arms sticking out of a polo shirt and spindly kid-legs in cloth shorts, throw itself into the woodchipper of bullies almost as if he received pleasure from doing so. Jude would sprint to Matt only when the fights were firmly over, Matt splayed on the ground like a cartoon failure, sometimes bloodied, but usually just smudged. Jude would stand over Matt and wonder how he could always look so happy. So at peace. When Jude would ask if Matt was alright, Matt would say, *I feel alive*. Jude didn't know what that meant yet, so he always asked and Matt would always say the same thing, *You'll understand when you're older*, though Jude was older than Matt. Jude was older now. He had been getting perpetually older since those moments and still he didn't understand. If anything he understood less and less. In wanting to understand, in wanting to prove his new life hadn't resigned him to ignorance, Jude stepped between Matt and the other boy, put his hands on both Matt's shoulders and tried to make him look away from the other boy. Matt's eyes were terrifying. Jude could see how relaxed they were. That they held no tension. They were Matt's happy eyes, the eyes he always used to have on during their childhood. Jude flinched and then felt Matt lifting him, moving him calmly to the side like Jude was one glass too many. Jude felt helpless. Embarrassed. Ashamed at how easily his body was made insignificant to the night. How little he knew about protection. He hoped Léa had been looking away at that moment and then he stepped back and let it happen, like always.

You can fuck right off.

Watch it *mate*. You don't want to embarrass yourself in front of all your pretty friends.

Would you two just kiss already? Jesus.

Matt and the boy were nose to nose and the scene made Marie recoil. Marie tried to look away but couldn't. Little lights on the bar's ceiling were tinkling off the boys' cheekbones. They looked pretty and blushed in glitter. Marie watched as Matt lifted his hands to the boy's face and then felt an old jealousy. She watched Matt's body flex and could imagine it flexing under all his clothes. She knew his torso, from having spent so much time pressed against it. Marie thought about the way it looked in blue water, the abstraction water gave it when half exposed and wading. Marie thought back to a summer when the group had borrowed a car, crammed in it and drove south to a rented house they all agreed they felt too young for, to do nothing but sit around in the sun for a week. She remembered Matt's body going brown, day by day, and she remembered Matt's hands taking to the emptiness of her cheeks, with different intentions. She remembered how happy Matt had looked in that week of nothingness and noticed the look had returned to him now, troublingly, in a moment of something so terrible. Embarrassing. Summer was only just over, and that made Marie more than jealous. It hurt her. Not having seen his body brown. A crack shot through the bar and Marie returned from her warmer thoughts, looking around trying to understand. First, Marie looked at the tree in the traffic circle, which was still standing. Then she looked at Rachel, who was clutching her face. Marie looked for Karim. Their bartender was always so calm, his expression a place she could escape to, for comfort. Karim's face was calm now, even as he dropped a glass and began running.

Matt stop.

Stop.

Stop Matt.

Matthieu. Arrête.

Arrête.

Stop.

Stop.

Eli watched and thought, *Boys*. He'd always loved the vulnerability in fighting. The love inherent in punching. If he could ever date a boxer, Eli would feel simultaneously nervous and safe. And also fully content. The fight pushed deeper into the bar. The fight bounced off the bar walls, rattling the giraffes, which looked on rockingly and without breaking eye contact. The force sparked many of Eli's more dormant fantasies. Eli watched the arms entangling and thought of gods and octopuses. Zeus as a swan. Zeus as a shower of gold. Zeus as Japanese erotica. The fantasies sent Eli squirming. He appreciated Matt in that moment, almost wanted him for having shed his months-long stupor and showed real emotion: a smile in the face of violence. Matt had the stranger by the scarf and pounded into him. The stranger dipped, flipped Matt into a choke hold, and returned his punches. The fight flowed. Eli thought of oceans and the holy sounds his friends made within them. He prayed the fight would keep going. But he saw Rachel step in between the two boys, her nose somehow already bleeding, and Eli knew the fight would be shortly over. That it needed to end for the sake of the circle. He knew fighting could change people in both good ways and bad, and he knew change, regardless of its quality, was not what was needed just now. Return was the needed deviation for the circle, not change. He saw Rachel put her back on Matt's chest and try to push them both away. He saw rogue throws clattering off Rachel's shoulders, so Eli moved closer, putting his hands into the waves. In the shrunken distance, Eli could see Matt's smile getting bigger with Rachel pressed against him. Eli, bigger than both Matt and the stranger, worked his size into the chaos, calming it, spreading it apart. It was fun, affecting a returning, forcing oneself between a natural magnetism, between the moon and its baitable ocean. The scene calmed Eli. He looked back and forth, the stranger panting and snarling. Matt panting and smiling, holding Rachel, both bloody and laughing. And so Eli was pleased, because the fight was over, and because Matt had gotten a taste of the only thing he'd ever wanted.

Tu as de la chance que tes potes soient là.

Fuck off, frog.

Make sure you keep that girl around to protect you.

I fucking will. Bet I will.

The other boy watched as Matt was dragged from the bar. The boy knew he'd won the fight. He'd gotten in the most punches and his face had barely been touched. He thought he might have even broken his opponent's nose. He'd felt it buckle under one of his punches. And yet *Matt,* his opponent, had been smiling the entire time. He'd heard the name repeated, ringing out over all of the screaming. Matt. He put the name in his mouth and said it. *Matt. Matthieu.* Through the windows, he could see Matt wrapped around with arms, petted, stroked, being calmed, his face being wiped. But the affection didn't seem necessary. Matt was laughing, and now his friends were laughing too. Even the bartender was smiling, wagging his finger at Matt like a secretly proud parent feigning authority. The boy looked at his own group of friends. They all looked so serious. They were all standing exactly where he'd left them, statuary in the face of responsibility. The boy looked at Matt again, cracked his neck and felt desire, for him, desire to be loved by so many others, loved while happily bleeding.

And outside, as it does on a cold evening, the round-about became a mountain town hidden between the sister peaks of Belleville and Ménilmontant. The waterfall down beneath Rue de Cascades could be heard crashing, muted beautifully, paved over as it was by Napoleon's cobblestones. A bohemian stumbled out of the more artistic bar, paused, and could see their breath. The man fighting the tree had tired and now lay slouched against its trunk mumbling. A group of friends, arm in arm, stumbled and set off from the bric-a-brac bar, though it could just have easily been a chalet. They slid together in one direction, limping, seemingly propping one another up.

Whenever we saw the protestors they were few and lightly shouting, on their way to somewhere else. They wore their yellow, but we never saw them smashing anything up. And we definitely never saw their revolution being put down by water cannons. Some of our friends made Saturdays of going out to get videos of the smashing and the spraying, way on the other side of town. They sent those videos around, so we saw it that way. But more often we heard the sounds of the struggling revolution in the distance, in the big public squares of the city, like a human thunder coming, a thunder that never came. One morning, we met for coffee in the Latin Quarter, for no better reason than to be somewhere fancier, somewhere with history. From the hill of that beautiful neighborhood, we could hear Place d'Italie going off, very far away, but its energy nearing. People coming up from the Place said it was going to be a big one. They said big one with their eyebrows raised. We saw the fancy neighborhood growing afraid, then getting ready. We watched a banker putting up plywood boards over his cash machine, next to a baker putting up plywood boards over her windows. The banker helped the baker and the baker helped the banker, and when they were done they thanked each other and both looked worried. We only understood why the banker should be worried about putting up his boards.

Jude and Léa have a happy baby

There's a story that still goes around about the round-about, which stands as a point of pride for the city. As the story goes, soon after the Occupation of Paris, when Göring arrived to purge France of its art, he heard rumor of a cache of masterpieces hidden in one of Paris's working-class hilltop neighborhoods. First he laid siege to Montmartre, drawn by the romantic idea that a treasure trove of Parisian history might be hidden in its most iconic of artistic locales, that hillside with its vineyard and its own ghosts. He looked with a passion, but Göring ultimately found nothing there. Further inquisition led him to suspect that the paintings in question—sometimes Matisses and Monets, sometimes Degas and Cézannes, depending on who was doing the telling—were being stored in an attic somewhere on or near Rue Levert. Thorough huntings for the spoil by the Nazi Reichsmarschall were met with equally thorough subterfuge on the part of the Bellevilloise Resistance, namely by way of rapid nighttime swapping of the artworks between apartments around the roundabout. In his four years of plunder, Göring sent over 25,000 railcars full of art from France to Germany, himself stealing nearly $200 million of paintings, sculptures, and artifacts, which he sent to his hunting lodge at Carinhall, but he never found the cache hidden up in Belleville. In the years that followed, people in the neighborhood liked

to say that together they drove Göring carsick, spinning
his Mercedes around the traffic circle, which they attest
to seeing him do on multiple occasions.

It just sounds so sexless.

What would you know about it?

It's not like it's a business.

It's the most respectful word. For everyone.

What would you call them then?

Un compagnon, peut-être?

Companion?

Maybe.

Jude listened, first to the conversation, then to the bully
inside his head. He watched the bob of Léa's shot glass,
saw it creep to her lips, then fall as she got distracted,
as she slurred her opinions into the conversation. Jude's
mind slurred. Each time Léa's shot dropped, it kissed the
soft crown of their son's head. More than the tequila, it
was that son who was making Jude slur. His. His little
apostrophe. The way his son cooed and reached, not for
his distracted mother, but for the shot in his mother's
hand. And then the way his mother, only Jude's girlfriend,
seemed to have no idea what she was holding or what
was being demanded of her. The repeated reaching and
stretching for a drink was acting like an elastic on reality,
snapping between what did and did not exist. The shots
existed, fully existed, Léa had taken five already, but this
one seemed to be making Léa happiest, to tease her to play
with it. The fights existed, he and Léa starting from pas-
sive aggressive, blowing right through aggressive, arriving

at flat-out screaming in seconds over who had done and not done what, the arguments reaching their climax with the not-so-subtle insinuations that both had wondered if maybe what they had created, together, would have been better off never having existed in the first place. In those moments, existence felt sickening and went fuzzy around the edges. In their silent moments after fighting, Jude would often think about how, stored within his body, lived the ability to create a soul. Or rather, half the ability. And the idea would make Jude shudder and send him running back to Léa, frantically apologizing, with no memory of what he needed to apologize for or what they'd even been fighting about to begin with. Jude looked at Léa, happy, with a much different face than she wore when she was angry, and Jude felt guilty. A warm, yellow-green guilt. A textured feeling for what he'd done to Léa. For having ruined her. Like he was the reason Léa kept failing to take her shot. Like he was the power getting in her way. Léa lifted the shot again. Dropped it again. And from the bar, where Jude stood holding his own shot, he nearly screamed.

Léa turned to Jude and smiled. He looked sad, and she felt guilty for what she'd done to him. Léa felt the weight in her lap and felt trapped by it, for Jude. Léa only wished that within the entrapment, Jude was having fun, just a little, even for just a moment. The spring evening was calm and warm. Perfect for just a little fun. She turned back to the circle. They were talking, but all their eyes were fixed on the weight in her lap, like they had been the entire night, and the attention was disconcerting. Léa told herself to feel proud, that this was progress. But thinking wasn't working. She hated that no one looked at Jude anymore. Sometimes people looked at Léa, to tell her how cute her baby looked. But no one looked at Jude and she hated that for him. He was interesting before he was a father. He'd had plans to invent solutions, and Leah thought back to the nights when they'd stay up late, looking at Jude's computer, with him showing her all the problems he could solve with it. And Léa remembers herself, how attractive she was on those evenings, listing off all the problems she wanted to solve, watching Jude be taken aback by her ambitions, watching him get excited at her using his tools. Léa remembered the nights when they would only have sex after they'd mentally exhausted themselves with planning, and the sex would be bad but meaningful. She looked down at her son and tried to remind herself that some of that man, from those evenings, was woven into him. But her son looked nothing like Jude. And he didn't look much like Léa either. Léa turned back to Jude and forced herself to smile, this time with teeth. She lifted the shot toward him, tried to remember what number it was, then took it. They took it together. Jude and Léa and no one else. Not even their child. Léa closed her eyes and felt a warm and dizzy freedom run all through her.

Boyfriend sounds so cheesy, no? They have a kid now.

No. Boyfriend is hot. It means more. It's more devious. It's more teenage.

That's exactly my point. It's not serious enough.

What if you've been together for ten years?

If you're not married, they're still your boyfriend.

But what if they're more than that?

And what if you're queer, and those words don't work for you?

Ils ne sont pas queer. Ça c'est sur.

More like dumb.

What?

Nothing.

Careful.

Marie shot out her arms and caught the baby as he tipped from Léa's lap. The baby looked up at her and laughed. Marie hated how casual Léa was as a mother. Barely holding on to her baby, letting the kid crawl wherever he wanted, taking shots. Their bar was not a playpen. There were sharps and sockets. There were drunks and losers. There was literally an alley out the back full of rats. Marie had already been a mother to her hard-packaged little sisters who found ways of getting hurt and crying constantly. So she knew. She knew the quick arrival of the danger. She'd only been fourteen then, when she became a stand-in mother, too young for the responsibility but old enough to recognize failings in people older than herself. The evening was looking too much like her own mother and father. The parents she had loved until they made her three siblings and then began to sour and rot and go to pieces. The baby reached for Marie's hair, got some and tugged it, but gently. The baby smiled and garbled happiness. Marie told herself to smile back, since he was her friends' kid, but couldn't bring herself to do so. Babies were always smiling at Marie, from high chairs and pushcarts, and baby bike seats wearing their oversized helmets, and she always made sure to return the look with one of cold reality. Her sisters had smiled at her, even when she scolded them. They were so small and vulnerable and without Marie, they probably would have starved. Now that her sisters were teenagers, they took care of themselves, just like Marie had trained them. They were hard and they asked little of Marie, which she appreciated. But sometimes she did think about them as babies. How they would come to her crying, curl up in her lap, and after some tickling or stroking, they would be soothed and they would laugh and they would reach up and try to kiss her on the cheek. Marie was sure that babies could not read her mind, or else they would never have smiled at her. If they could read her mind, they would have heard her mocking them and repeating her mantra that she would never have one herself. She convinced herself constantly. No matter how many babies smiled at Marie, she would never have one, even if they always laughed and calmed in her hands.

Why not just friend?

What are you, seventy-two? Did you just move to a care home?

I just mean that a single word shouldn't be necessary.

But it's a good word. It means you're combined.

It means you're equal.

Marie passed Matt the baby and he stiffened. Matt saw Marie notice. He put the baby on his knee and bounced

him like he'd seen on television. The baby grimaced so
Matt stopped. Now he didn't know what to do with him.
With inaction, the baby made oppressed noises and Matt
wondered what it was about Marie that made the baby
giggle. She hadn't bounced him. She hadn't done much of
anything specific. He wanted to make the baby giggle and
he liked that Marie could. She wasn't casual about holding
the baby, but she didn't show much interest either. She just
spoke to him in adult words every now and then, which
seemed to work fine. Not like Léa, who was good with
the kid, but was constantly obsessing over him, cooing at
him in falsetto, inciting mild anxiety in others. Jude was
good with the baby too, but in a different way. When Jude
held him, Matt noticed the baby begin to mimic, with
Jude's sense of authority growing, and the room filling
with a stronger air of solutions. Matt liked Jude as a father,
how he seemed to so easily teach the baby, for example,
how to use a spoon, then how to put that spoon in his
mouth. Jude's life was always so perfectly put together,
even while living so far from home. Jude never struggled
to learn the language. Jude never had to fight to find a
job. Matt wondered if those skills were genetic. If Jude
would have to teach them to his son or if they were already
hard-wired in, if the little thing he was now holding was
already better at caring for himself than Matt was in his
late twenties. The thought made him nervous about his
failings, his uselessness, and what his genes looked like.
He assumed he'd someday become a father, but he never
imagined what that reality would demand back from him

or what it would take without his asking. The baby began to cry quietly. Matt looked up and tried to find Jude, who was sitting at the bar, speaking to Karim. Matt could see that Jude was drunk and he watched Jude trying to make a point, leaning deep in his barstool and slowly tipping from it, stumbling and crashing to the floor. Matt passed Sarah the baby and ran over to him. Jude was curled up, giggling. He tried helping Jude up, but Jude just repeated, *I feel alive*, which Matt didn't understand. Matt set himself down on the floor with Jude, stroking his head. He felt the evening becoming a daycare, the traffic circle hazy in the steamy windows, lights from outside turning merry-go-round in the glass, their giggles bouncing off walls, their sound of immanence, and their potential to turn sad very quickly.

Leave him, he's fine.

The word makes it sound like there's a contract.

Obviously there's no contract.

Do you and Jude have certain contractual obligations?

No.

Are you starting a start-up?

Fuck off.

Well then why would you call someone that?

Where are you going?

Sarah thought about Léa's specific word while Léa stood, wobbly, and asked Eli for two cigarettes. She crossed the room, taking two knees beside Jude. She bent herself oddly and nuzzled his chest with the crown of her head. Jude stood right up, fast and sturdy, like he'd never been down in the first place. Léa was a good mother, Sarah thought.

She knew when and when not to care. Like when she had all her friends around her. Sarah watched as Léa and Jude went outside together and smoked, manically puffing the cigarettes like they were too young to smoke. Sarah looked down at the kid's face in her lap and didn't see any of Jude or Léa in him. Then she looked at Pierre's face and wondered what his and hers would look like combined. If the creature would be furry or smooth. If it would grow straight or have scoliosis. If it would be sturdy on its feet. The thoughts felt like unnecessary failures of giving in. All Sarah wanted was her garden. For the garden to take on her and Pierre's faces. Bushy rosemary. Sharp acacias. Soft boxwood. Kind roses. Natural grapes and ancient grains. Purple carrots and geometric cabbages. She only wanted for their garden to birth them cornucopias. Pierre and Sarah hadn't been in the city for three weeks and before taking the train in at the afternoon, specifically to be with their best friends' child the first time he went to the bar, the amount of time away from Paris had worried her. Like she wouldn't understand its concrete and flesh. And she hadn't. The city had leaned in around her, like it had when she was younger, the buildings all cleaving inward making jambon sandwiches out of all the pudgy bodies who were foolish enough to live in such an inhumane place. She was happy for Jude and Léa, happy to see them letting off steam, but she could see the night was only beginning and all she wanted was for her and Pierre to go home, take off their clothes, lie free in the garden, and make it healthy. She wanted to try her best at becoming turf so that she might better understand it. Because the plants she'd tried growing already had been dying so fast and so violently. Sarah said a long *fuck* under her breath about it. Another failed spring would push the business plan back yet another year. But Sarah was strong. She convinced herself it would get better, her garden out there in the countryside, alone without her. She passed the kid to Pierre, noticed how he looked more like Pierre than like Jude, then asked herself what the hell was wrong with her. She was beyond that sort of thinking.

Pierre lifted the baby up and threw him to the air, like to God. Like a cherub to heaven. Like Cupid up to love on high. Pierre caught the baby and the baby made soft noises. Pierre nuzzled soft noises back into the baby's softer stomach. He saw, out the window, Jude sliding down the hood of a car he was balancing on, Léa struggling to prop him up. Pierre felt a pang of anger and embarrassment run through his arms, so he squeezed the baby tighter, pretending the baby was his. He didn't want this life for Sarah or for anyone, except, at moments when he felt lonely, maybe for himself. It was a truth he'd never told Sarah, for fear. The fear wasn't financial, or anything like that. Pierre and Sarah already had more than they would ever need, in order to have or to have not. The fear was in regards to hope and the ability to chase it. He felt proud to support Sarah's dream for the freedom to explore herself. Prouder still for the fact that, from a family that had been beholden to work, he had created a world in which he was free to earn when he liked, move where he wanted, and live as far from society as he saw fit. But these accomplishments didn't relieve him of his body and what it now seemed to itch for. A copying. A beautiful doubling. A mystical summoning of new matter. Matter, however, that survived on freedom. Pierre calculated how each new living human removed no fewer than two people's endowed freedom to be. People were born containing multiples of restriction within them. Pierre's understanding was being made into reality now with how the baby had made Jude less futuristic. Pierre and Jude didn't talk like they used to about starting something. Jude didn't stay up for late nights of dreaming in tiny apartments. He didn't talk of quitting his job and joining Pierre to invent something important. There was never the ringing of their refracted phrase, *Let's fucking do it then*. And then again, Jude had quit all that long before he and Léa had got pregnant. Before Pierre and Sarah had even moved away. Pierre knew that.

Do you think they're alright?

Of course. They just need a night off.

At least they're acting like partners.

In crime, maybe.

It's a terrible word.

Relax. They haven't really been drinking in months.

More like years.

They're just easy drunks now.

Speak for yourself.

How do they say it in your rudimentary language, *a cheap date*?

Pierre forced the baby onto Eli's lap, saying it was his

turn. Eli cringed and held the baby with only fingertips.
Eli hated the baby for the way it sobered his friends. Or
apparently, just those who weren't the baby's parents. The
circle had barely been drinking save Jude and Léa and Eli
tried to make a face at the baby to show how much he
hated it. The baby put its hands on Eli's forearms, pulled
itself closer until it was curled heavy on Eli's chest. Eli
remembered the hum that lived in his own father's chest,
a memory he couldn't get rid of. Eli's father would always
hum fisherman songs from the west. Sometimes Eli heard
the songs sung on the Métro, going home alone, late, sung
by groups of drunk boys Eli fantasized over. He never knew
the words, but he knew the melodies, and he would hum
them back on his side of the Métro platform. Sometimes
he considered crying, alone on late trains home, because
the image felt beautiful and dramatic to him. He never
could manage tears though. Just pitiful faces he checked
in the mirror. The baby lifted his head up and down
against Eli's chest, thumping a baseline to the song. Eli
remembered his father's mustache. The sound it made
when his father sang, lips tickling the coarse follicles. Eli
wondered if his father still had facial hair. Whether he
might hear it coming someday before even seeing it. If that
might be how he recognized him. Eli collected himself. He
thought of the downy cheeks and thick lips of every boy
he'd ever loved. Always with hair. The hair, always capable
of soft symbols. The baby squeezed Eli with a surprising
strength and Eli whispered *I hate you, Eli* into the baby's
ear even though Eli was not the baby's name. The baby

laughed, uncontrollably laughed. Eli grinned, then began to hum, just to try it.

We've got to cut them off.

Who's going to take them home?

Not me.

They're fine. They'll be fine.

Come on. Think of the kid.

He was their decision.

Putain, you're soulless.

Rachel lifted the baby by his armpits and turned him squirming, the motion awkward. The baby grimaced. She wanted the baby. Wanted to make him laugh and attempt talking. Seeing Léa growing, becoming more and more beautiful, had made Rachel jealous. She tickled the baby's middle and blew small raspberries against his cheeks. The doting only made the baby grimace more. Rachel said, *Oh come on*, then tried inverting him, rocking gently. The baby choked, sputtered air, and began moaning. Rachel stopped rocking but the moaning broke to wailing. The circle looked up and Rachel started shrinking. She saw Matt watching her and smiling, Marie judging, Pierre and Sarah looking ambivalent, Eli exhaling. Rachel looked down at her lap and saw light green on her pants. She felt the warm of it against her leg. She gagged and instinctually put the baby to the floor. There was immediate motion. Jude and Léa were running behind her, laughing, tripping, and sprawling on the ground with their child. Marie matched them, pushing through chairs and diving on the floor. Laughter and anger were mixing together and Rachel was bent up by the difference. She closed her eyes and wanted the past. She wanted Marie and Sarah and Léa to be alone, talking about books and movies and potential futures that all three of them had known would never become a reality. She wanted each one to repeat the advice they used to beat into one another, *Never become a mother*. Rachel knew that being a mother meant becoming a parent and she knew full well the danger in that sort of becoming.

Jesus. What are you doing?

What?

Look. Do you have any more diapers?

Any more what?

Fucking diapers, Léa.

Shit. No. I don't think so.

Really?!

What?! I'm sorry.

Also on Rue Levert, at the bottom of the stairs that connect the quaint pedestrian street with the busier Rue des Pyrénées thirty-four steps above, there is a resigned cast-iron plaque fixed to the wall of the school that fills the entire north side of the passage. The plaque iron ore was sourced from existing stock drawn from a mine found high in the Pyrenees mountains, near the border with Spain and Andorra. In the winter, the plaque gets cold. In the summer, when the late afternoon sun works its way into the road, the plaque gets hot. And sometimes, in the spring, a small bouquet of marguerites in plastic wrapping is placed in a cast iron ring bored into the stones below the plaque. The person who places the bouquet is rarely caught in the act. Just as well. It's not graffiti. The bouquet of flowers will hang in its ring until it dies, after usually around two weeks, at which point the plaque is left by itself for another year. The plaque must then speak to itself alone. And the plaque is known to repeat itself. It often says, *A la mémoire des élèves de cette école déportés de 1942 à 1944 parce que nés juifs, victimes innocents de la barbarie Nazie et du gouvernement Vichy. Ils furent exterminés dans les camps de la mort. Plus de 1000 de ces enfants vivaient dans le 20eme. Ne les oublions jamais.*

Thick black smoke rose off the church, turning green in the evening. It was pretty, unfortunately. And it had poison in it, we were told later. We had seen the smoke from across the city, just like everyone says you will in fiction. We rushed to get to it. We paid for Métro tickets to get there faster. We grew impatient at how long it was taking. We almost argued even, from how badly we wanted to see history. We thought the history might only last a second, but it didn't. When we got there, we moved closer, closer, until we were as close as we could get. Close enough to breathe in the poison, we were told later. We didn't know we were in danger then because so many people were doing it too, breathing in, watching, mesmerized by the white-hot triangle in the burning eaves, white in the pink burning evening. The others around us on the Pont de la Tournelle were just as burning and it made them do funny things too. Some grown men were crying and singing. Some grown women were singing and laughing. Everyone was singing at least, and doing a lot of breathing in. Everyone had out their telephones, singing while holding up telephones, divvying up history and taking some of it with them. We did it too, with our phones. And we sang. And no one we knew ever replayed the videos we each took then because they were always the same. They never changed. The church just kept on burning.

Marie feels bad but can't say how

Down the lower portion of Rue de la Mare, the road hooks past a community theater designed for one-man shows, then temporarily becomes a bridge of corrugated steel. Beneath the bridge runs the disused urban belt railway system. Just past the bridge, the train tracks disappear into a tunnel running into the hillside, the tunnel pointed back in the direction of the roundabout, though nearly two hundred feet below it. Covering the tunnel is a tight-fitting door made of a mixture of sheet metal and chain link fencing. The fencing lets the tunnel breathe. From the bridge, one can see only a few feet into the guts of the city, for the light dies quickly in its gape. Some say that behind the door, ever since this section of the railway's closure in the 1930s, generations of Parisians have been born and died knowing only a subterranean life, their front steps Ménilmontant and their backyard Buttes Chaumont, where, if traveling counterclockwise, the tunnel takes its next breath of air. Some say these Parisians are related to the mole people living under New York City's Riverside Park. Something like cousins. Others say these Parisians have become accustomed to the comings and goings of those on the hillside above them, their neighbors whose presence they keep abreast of through vibrations, which are said to even convey emotions, like a pinging for sadness, or a scratching for joy. If it is to be believed, the Parisians lower down are thought to know what's coming next for those above, but unfortunately not for themselves.

Sadly, there was always a face behind a beard. Karim knew that from having served twenty years of beards, beer flowing through them. Two decades of bar ownership had made Karim hard to the shorn truth of a face, to the truth no amount of hair could cover up. Karim knew that beards were good to mask the violence foretold above the lips and below jawbones. More, he knew that eyes were good for nothing. That eyes could be batted and winked. Karim had seen too many pretty-eyed fighters who wouldn't blink before striking a woman down. Karim knew, on his life, that reality existed in the lower half of the face, where the tremors of pain were stored and waiting to be returned to the shortsighted world. Karim had been around long enough. He knew. And when he saw this new beard approach his bar, with a left hand holding up a single finger and a right hand lightly stroking Marie's back, he winced, then put on a smile. Karim was a good bartender before anything else. As he poured the stranger's beer, he looked out the window of his bar, the reliable view, the same he'd had for twenty years. Gas exhaust was cooking in the traffic circle, stinking. Men and their dogs were lingering along its edges, trying not to breathe in the heat too deeply, blowing out smoke and wiping off temple sweat with the backs of their smoking hands. The previous night had been cool and evenly spaced but then in the morning, the heat arrived to fill the spaces. Now the heat maintained the space and slowed the spin of the evening.

It was the week of false summer that comes in spring, with its terrible heat, exciting but premature. Karim knew it well because it came every year. It was a heat that led to binge drinking, the sort that made Karim rich, but that he hated nonetheless for its consequences.

Nathan, everyone. Everyone, Nathan.

Hey Nathan.

Ça va Nathan?

Nice to meet you.

You alright?

Enchanté.

Nice to meet everyone.

How's it going?

Très bien. I've heard so much about you all.

Nathan sat down in an empty space on the banquette, filling the friendship circle's biggest gap. He moved around in the space much like a dog getting comfortable. The bar was cooler than the world outside and Nathan seemed to relax too quickly in the space. He began to make a humming noise and waited. Sarah had always been the best at starting conversations with strangers, asking them approachably meaningful questions, lulling them into comfort. Sarah had learned it from her family, at dinner with all the important people who needed to be made to feel more important. She'd often wondered what her circle talked about with new people when she wasn't around, if the group appeared different to the world without her there to lead its inquisitions. Sarah worried her friends wouldn't seem interesting or interested enough without her, dying on the hill of routine getting-to-know-you questions. Her questions weren't only for vanity though. They were for protection, strategically designed to expose weakness and corruption. Like a spy hunter, Sarah liked to imagine. Sarah heard her phone buzz against the kitchen counter and she read Rachel's message, which felt hot in her hand. It said, *This guy is super cute. And he seems nice too.* Sarah replied, *Ask him what he was doing just before getting to the bar. Tell me what he says.* Sarah looked out the window to her yard and the forest behind it. The sunset was pinkish, with a splash of orange. The sky looked good as a setting for the blue and white flowers of her garden and she could see her bees skipping between the flowers. A hawk circled and Sarah watched it, then grew impatient and looked back at Rachel's message. Sarah wrote, *So?* but she would get no reply the rest of the evening.

Pierre took his place next to Sarah at the counter and put a confident chop through a soft tomato, the gummy seeds squirting onto the polished tiles. Out the window, the young tomato plants were wilting in the surprising heat, but Pierre didn't want to think about that or tell Sarah. *Did you get Rachel's message too?* was all he said. Pierre pushed the seeds into a little pile with the side of his palm, licked juice off, and wondered if the new boy would be funny. Pierre wanted to know if the new boy would make his jokes for him, keep the mood light and devious. He knew his friends could be dry without him there to break the ice, sacrificing himself with dad jokes. Pierre hoped the new boy could make Marie laugh easily, and for the rest of the circle to smile at Marie finally laughing. Usually, when Marie brought new boys around, it reminded Pierre of the day after Marie had first slept with someone, so much later than the rest of their high school friends, and the group at the time had applauded. Marie had bowed but she hadn't smiled and Pierre could see that something about it wasn't right and so the applause had broken his heart, though he had himself applauded. Pierre was glad to be done with those moments and so instead he thought about Nathan and tried to imagine his face telling a story. He thought that maybe the new boy could be funnier than he was. Pierre wanted him to be funnier, even though the thought made him jealous. He imagined Matt and Jude slapping the boy on the back and saying, *Nice one, whatcha drinking, round on me*, in their perfect accents. Pierre felt the cool beer of a good laugh sliding down his throat. He felt his hot throat being cleared by the cold beer and imagined saying to the boy, *Mec, on dirait que tu rends Marie très heureuse*. He stopped cutting and opened the refrigerator, the cool air bashing into his naked thighs. He shifted things around but there were no beers inside.

Il est très mignon ton bébé. Il a quel âge?

Thanks man. Almost one and a half.

No, almost two. *Et merci.*

Wow.

He looks so much like both of you. An even mix.

You think?

Yeah.

You might be the first person to ever say that.

So how did you two meet?

On the apps. Did Marie not tell you the story?

Yeah, she told us.

So I heard you two have a really nice garden? I actually grew up on a rosemary farm. It was super nice actually.

No, that's Pierre and Sarah. They're the ones I told you live in the countryside. This is Jude and Léa.

Ah, pardon.

Don't worry about it.

Is there even such a thing as a rosemary farm?

There is.

Just rosemary.

Que du romarin.

Léa handed Nathan her child. She wanted to test him. She wanted to see Marie's face with Nathan holding a baby, to see if there was any potential in it. Nathan turned the baby around with confidence and held him facing out, back against Nathan's chest, so the baby could see the circle and be more of an adult. Léa liked that. Then Nathan tickled the baby under his armpits so the baby squealed with happiness, which Léa obviously enjoyed. She waited for Nathan to tell her something about the baby that he thought she might not know. He didn't, and Léa liked that most. She looked at Marie, who had on an absent smile, like she was at peace. Léa smiled at Marie. Léa had gotten in the habit of timing days like weeks, watching hours with patience, seeing how much change could take place in a minute. Seconds passed, and Léa saw Nathan as an aging man, giving Marie advice and taking just as much back from her, good and clear advice on being happy with a child, which Marie always seemed to give, advice that was harsh in the present but was almost always correct, years and minutes later. What she imagined was nothing like Sarah and Pierre, who had turned out to be terrible with her son. Even with all their space, they refused to look after him, constantly avoiding her insinuations. Léa had begun to wonder if they weren't purposefully trying to rile him up when they were around, to show they were bad stand-in parents, so that she and Jude would stop asking them for help. Léa wanted help. She wanted a break. She imagined herself on a beach, just Jude and her for days of peace, for a real vacation. A vacation in Corsica or Menorca or Sardinia. One of the cheap and less popular European islands. A vacation where they were relaxed the entire time. Where they got in every moment of relaxation and she could return recharged for motherhood. Léa imagined herself taking off a bikini, putting on something comfortable, and taking a plane home where they knew Marie and Nathan had been looking after their kid for a week, teaching him how to give good advice and whatever else Nathan might be good at. It didn't really matter.

Jude saw Léa smiling and felt relaxed. More than relaxed; relieved. Jude could tell Léa liked Nathan and so did he. Or, at least, he had a good impression. Jude was nearly thirty and he hadn't made a new friend in at least three years. Instead, he'd lost many friends in the last years, some violently and some by attrition. The group was all Jude had left, and even it was shrinking.

Pierre rarely responded to his messages, except when they required no action. Then he responded right away. It wasn't that Jude feared spending time alone. He just felt too young for it now. Jude felt desperate not to stop learning from life. He'd been wanting new catalysts in his life for months now. Challenges to test him. He didn't want his life to change or become harder but he wanted new, microscopic problems he could ponder. Ideally, tiny problems in the form of interpersonal dramas that he could help in solving. Nathan had ropey, thin arms. They looked strong. They were connected to soft fingers and he thought that was probably good. Nathan was tall, with expressive shoulders, which he also thought was a good sign. Jude looked at Nathan's beard, something Jude could not grow, and associated Nathan with being manly, whatever that meant. He wondered if Nathan was respectful and hoped Nathan wasn't but that he could be. That he could learn to be, if Jude pushed him, if Jude told him, *Do better*, or *I swear to fucking God*. Even if there was nothing Jude could do about it or swear to. A hot wind from the open door caught Jude across the back of the neck and Jude thought, this is nothing, this is bearable. He felt so nearly thirty, at the perfect age to use his kid aggression for adult motivations. Jude didn't want to miss the chance. Nathan smiled at Jude and winked and that caught Jude off guard. Jude tried to smile back but Nathan had turned away.

You must be Matt.

Yep.

How are you?

I'm fine.

What do you do?

Hm?

What do you do?

I work.

Bon. I heard you got into a fight here, a couple years ago. I heard you really gave it to the guy.

I hope that's not all you've heard.

Of course not. I've heard other things.

Good things?

Very good things, of course.

Matt remembered where he'd been and where he wasn't now. He could feel the squeeze of the past, hotter than the night outside, and more humid. Matt remembered pushing himself in and out of the past, when it was the present, the present making him scream and want more presents for the future. He stared at Nathan and could imagine exactly how he was feeling. How hot the future-present must be for him, the infinitive against his bare skin. The *-ai*, the *-a*, and the *-ons*, whispered in his ear. Matt studied Nathan's subtle actions, moving Marie's wine glass back from the dangerous spot on the table where she always placed it, a lip hanging off the edge, pushing Marie's chair over when she got up so that when she came back she could be closer to her friends, picking Marie's phone up off the floor when she dropped it and not even glancing at the screen to see if there were any messages from someone else. Nathan was already doing everything Marie had asked Matt to be better at. Being considerate. Being less needy. Not being jealous. Being better. Marie aside, Nathan was doing great in the circle and that troubled Matt the most. The prick was making the circle laugh, relax their shoulders, and ask more questions. Nathan was prompting them to tell stories Matt had never heard. Stories of their childhoods. Stories of their defining moments. And worst, stories of how they overcame themselves for the better. Nathan was pulling the circle back into a past when they were happier and more excited. A living past in the present, like a cleansing. Matt felt a surge run through his muscles, like a death throe. A death by accepting that the reality of now is how the world was always destined to be. It felt like being a child, getting trapped in a wave and barreled. A wave death, or maybe a crashing baptism. Matt took a sip from Marie's glass of wine without anyone noticing. He held the liquid in his mouth a long time before swallowing, tasting the Carignan tannins of a long-dead savior.

So, Rachel, I've heard you're the wise one in the group?
Le quoi?
Le sage.
Says who? Did Marie say that?
No. Call it a feeling.
What would have given you that impression?
I can just tell.
Definitely better at giving advice than following it.
Maybe we can trade some then.
Rachel had recently been wondering if, had their friend group formed five years before it actually had, would they

have become a group of friends in the first place? She
doubted it. They would have had different faces and she
knew that a person's face made all the difference. They
would have been louder and quieter. They would have
needed differently. In the face of a new Nathan, Rachel's
question was morphing. If any Nathan entered the circle
now and stayed, would it be conceivable that they could
survive alongside each other for another half-decade?
She could already see how Nathan was changing Matt,
making him uncomfortable and falsely attentive. It lifted
his eyebrows and softened his edges. She liked it, but she
knew it was unsustainable. A Matt with greater effort
would become a harsh and obsessive person. A new Jude
too stern, too paternal. A new Léa, too calm and accepting.
Any Eli with less attention would grow fat and become
depleted. Pierre and Sarah would remain the same, due
to their distance, but their consistency would stand as an
unforgivable reminder of a different time, even if it wasn't
necessarily a better one, and the group would be forced to
stop seeing Pierre and Sarah altogether. And what about a
new Rachel? She remembered herself five years ago: better
skin and tackier fashion. Less awareness, bigger hair, and
thus, more decisive. She didn't want that life again, to
relive the mistakes she'd made by being sure. Rachel knew
that new people forced her to be sure. And to decide.
She was scared at the thought of stepping out from the
bar in the years to come, into false-summer nights, and
forgetting that she'd been turned into a Nathan Rachel.
A Rachel who looked wise and made decisions without

reflection, because that sort of Rachel was wiser and expected to be sure. Rachel could see herself in five more years—kid, partner—speaking entirely in statements. She hated the idea that she might ever like Nathan.

And you must be Eli, life of the party?

I don't know if I'd put it that way.

You look really familiar.

Really?

You don't live by Richard-Lenoir, do you?

Not at all.

Do you spend time there?

Not really.

Do you ever go to that bar, Le 17? The one with the good dancing.

Never.

Jamais?

Jamais.

Really? I could have sworn I'd seen you there.

The people there are really cool.

Must have been me in a different life.

We should go. The dancing is really great. I think you'd love it.

Someday, sure.

We could even have a dance-off.

Eli had always wanted to go to Le 17. He'd been told the bar had an accepting crowd and good music. He imagined himself different, with a different group of friends, one that went to Le 17 every Friday instead of the bar they always went to. He pictured himself dancing, then grinding, then kissing and touching the other patrons in the corners of doorways down roads he didn't know the names of or even recognize. He could feel the freedom of losing his reputation, becoming responsible for a new one he could ruin and ruin and start again. He was jealous of Nathan drinking in a bar he'd never been to, surrounded by strangers whose perceptions were soft and malleable. He already knew the sort of phrases he'd say at Le 17. Phrases like, *Houellebecq is as good as common street garbage you illiterate donkey*, even though Eli had never read any Houellebecq and had a feeling he would probably like him. Things like, *You call that dancing you ham-footed bitch*. Things like, *Relax, we're only just getting started*. Eli loved the idea of himself at Le 17 and doubly loved the fact that Nathan thought he'd seen him there. He stared at Nathan's squared-off cheekbones and as he did, as he imagined it at Le 17, Nathan's face came into focus. It became a friend's face. One he'd put his cheek to and leaned on after a night of too much rum. *How many Ti' punches is that for you? One too many darling*. Nathan's face began populating, reproducing more faces, morphing into boys and girls whose faces would have to be kissed or spanked to induce even more dancing. Their names would be Olympe and Aude, Alessandro and Amandine, Estelle, Blaise, Henriette, and whatever names he could think of that were most sinful. His name would be Jean Baptiste. And their personalities would be a reflection of his own, bouncing his ambitions back at him, making him do dance moves he'd never done, making him smell different and taste differently, making him into the person he was always supposed to be. Eli felt a light sweat break along his cheekbones, the tiny droplets thankfully caught and masked within his beard. He touched his beard and then beaded the wetness between his fingers. The sensation of the sweat on his fingertips was exciting. It reminded him of the best nights he'd ever had. And then Eli remembered exactly where he'd met Nathan before.

You're all so lucky to have Marie as a friend.

What do you mean?

I just mean that sometimes I wish I'd met her randomly. In another life. That we'd been friends.

That's a bit weird.

Quoi?

Nothing.

Right.

She just speaks of you guys so kindly. It must feel really special.

Yeah, I guess it does.

Marie didn't care what her friends thought about Nathan, but she did care what they were thinking about her, now, with her body so close to his. Nathan was just a body in time, but one that refracted. One that lit things up by play-acting. She knew she was better-looking in his presence, in the eyes of the world. Better-looking under the influence of appearing wanted, a reality Marie had always hated when witnessing it bolster and Botox the faces around her. Marie knew what Nathan was attempting to do. Kill her. With kindness and softer niceties, with attention, then tricking her into obsession by pulling back, conjuring addiction out of insecurity. He was French. The act was a given. Matt had never thought to try such a game. But she was enjoying her own role in it too, with Nathan, in the Parisian theater of a random fuck that for the French was somehow, someway, always capable of slipping easily into a soul-destroying love. She enjoyed playing oblivious to the awaiting cruelty. Feigning how unbelievable it was, them getting along so well. She liked using her eyes to imply she was fighting, hard, not to say she loved him too quickly. Marie could see how much Nathan loved her doing that. They'd met up six times, had sex six times, and every time ended with sickeningly passionate cuddling. Before messaging Nathan, asking him to come with her to the bar, she'd nearly written that she didn't think *this* was working out. But that wasn't a French thing to say. Then Marie began to wonder if she could manipulate her feelings by placing Nathan in front of the public, rather than having to watch him fuck her, alone, with his socks on like he liked to. Sometimes even with his scarf on. Marie wanted to see if, by showing herself to the circle with Nathan beside her, with her appearing happy, they'd treat her as if she was. Marie studied the circle's faces. Beyond the happy eyes, she could see Nathan was prompting jealousy and pride. Acceptance and reflection, individual self-assessment. But nothing related to her. She could tell they liked Nathan. That they would envelop him. And how that would be the worst for her. Marie exhaled and felt the dull yet painful yawn of bleakness. The feeling of something very important being almost perfect but not quite right. She decided to look at herself in all the reflections she could find, off windows and glasses. Off eyes. She made a huge smile and in the reflections she could see the corners of her lips turning down. Marie had been cursed with a frowning smile and she knew it. So Marie giggled, though no one had said anything funny. She looked at Nathan's legs, skinny as a secret under his tight jeans, and she put a hand on his inner thigh and squeezed it. He looked at her like she was interrupting him, and she mouthed, *On y va*. Marie stood and said her goodbyes fast so as not to have to kiss anyone in the group. She knew they would find it brusque and then she imagined what everyone was thinking.

As Marie and Nathan cut a diameter across the roundabout, they paused for a moment. Standing in front of the artistic bar's terrace was an Édith Piaf impersonator, far too tall for the part, halfway through a rendition of "Non, je ne regrette rien." She was being booed. Marie pulled Nathan away and they became yet another couple in the Parisian evening. The crowd around the singer, however, grew and became more savage, but the singer persisted, stamping her feet to the rhythm. She was blonde, though the dirt matted in her hair made her near enough a brunette, and she stank, her smell seeming to mount alongside her song's crescendo. She agitated the crowd like a car's honk on a calm Parisian Sunday. Some simply threw their hands in the air, while others began making exasperated sounds not dissimilar to baboons. The song began to physically assault the crowd and they reacted as such, calling her a whore, a dirty whore, and the son of a whore, though the insults rang impotent in the face of the music. For a moment, the impersonator paused, collecting herself. Then she began to stomp her foot again and when she let out the first notes of "La vie en rose," the crowd was nearly thrown from their feet. Some began to scream, mainly men, that she was degrading a French icon. That she was a blight on Piaf's legacy. Fewer women screamed, though they did move closer, insulting the singer's looks and the state of her decay, one even putting a finger to the singer's chest and telling her to go back wherever she came from, dirty son of a stinking whore. Eventually the rabble grew loud enough that they drowned out the music and they continued screaming, failing to notice the impersonator had abruptly quit singing. Surrounded, quiet, the impersonator smiled as she continued tapping the song's rhythm with her foot, conducting the terrace's anger. She was nearly home. She was letting her loved ones know she was soon in coming.

Word went around that it would be the hottest day on record.
Words such as oven *and* skin-cooking *were used. An idea was*
floated about death in the shade. An idea to visit Paris-Plages
was nixed. The city shut down. Parisians were told to go home.
We were worried for ourselves at first, but the worries were just
jealousies, hatred of our friends with pools in the countryside.
Besides, we remembered there was beer. At a cafe, one of us
brought up the heat island, and for doing so they were summarily
flayed. Instead we decided to wait out the heat near the cold beer
taps because beer was all we needed. Around three, with the heat
at its peak, the elderly arrived and looked terrified. They sat
in the shade and drank water. One of us said we could feel our
skin cooking and the rest of us laughed. We agreed it was a new
feeling. We laughed until we looked a second time at our elders,
then nothing was funny again. They were panting. They looked
up at their apartments on the high floors of the buildings. They
had nowhere to go, nowhere to escape to, not into beer, not even to
their homes. One of our elders lifted himself and trudged across the
street to a corner store. He came back with two boxes of ice pops.
The kind that change colors as you lick them. He offered around
the pops to his friends and they regretfully accepted. No one smiled
or thanked him. They just licked and looked up at their windows.
We watched the treats change colors in their mouths, giving their
lips a rainbow lipstick. The old man turned to us without smiling,
his ice pop cerulean in its final phase. He lifted the box full of pops
to us and said, S'il vous plait, *but we refused. The old man looked*
angry and insisted, so we accepted.

Eli repeats his favorite story

In the winter, in the hillside cirque where the roundabout sits, a fog can get socked in so thick that strangers step out from within it. The tall streetlights on Rue de la Mare are not strong enough to see their own feet and the gentle switchbacks of Rue des Cascades turn to blind and dangerous corners. In the summer it's the haze that thickens, with the heat radiating up from the low urban plain, the flatland full of tourists breathing and trucks idling and the last of the old artisans dumping chemicals into the gutters with their knotty hands. On the hottest Paris days, the pollution presses down to the elevation of Belleville and Ménilmontant, down on the roundabout, and the air becomes a thickness you must fight your way through. On those days, people from the neighborhood struggle to the top of Belleville Park to see the dirty air turn the sunsets red as blood, as if God was performing a shameful ritual. It is only then, usually, when the sun is fully set and blue is deafening the red in the sky, that the air over Paris is finally set free and a blow sets in across the hillside, cooling it quickly. It is when the wind doesn't come and the heat presses down on those trying to sleep that the summers on the hillside become dangerous and the roads on the hillside seem to narrow.

Eli, tell Nathan about the time you went to Dover.

Matt rolled his eyes. Eli noticed.

Should I?

Come on. Please.

It's so long though.

But it's such a good story.

Tell it. *Allez*.

Eli felt himself as the main character in his own fiction and the feeling felt good. He let himself be taken by the cool feeling of it running over his feet, climbing up his thighs. Outside, the air was hot, but the fiction was refreshing.

Alright, so. This happened in a February. Jesus, eight years ago now. So I decided to go backpacking around England, to see castles and maybe see if English boys were anything like they pretended to be in stories. I was staying in London with a friend who'd moved there for university, and I was supposed to go north for a few days, up to the Lake District. But the weather was really bad there and I got an email from the hotel I'd booked saying they'd decided to close. Because of the storm. So, I looked for other places to visit. It was my first trip on my own, so it felt like it meant something, you know? Like if I would have just stayed in London, I would have failed myself. *Tu sais ce que je veux dire?*

Oui, je comprends.

The embellishment made space for Eli to move around. He looked down on his fictional self as the fiction rushed in and he made himself swim in the space that his telling created. He could feel the fiction rising over his back and taking over his neck.

You have to understand that I studied English. That I was training to become an English literature professor at the time, so everything was very Johnson and Dickens, if you know what I mean. Everything was very Hardy. I didn't know where to go and I stared out the window at the black clouds rolling in over London. They became my inspiration. Because of the storm I got this idea to live out my Lear kink and go to Dover. To throw myself from the cliffs in a fit of madness.

What a romantic you are, Eli.

More like a dandy.

More like a cad.

You don't even know what cad means.

So I found some tickets on the bus for like, ten pounds or whatever and I found a hostel online that said it had space. I booked the bus and the hostel and went to the bus station. Victoria Station. It was three p.m. and the trip was supposed to take three hours with a stop in Canterbury.

This story is so crazy Nathan. You're not going to believe it.

Eli felt the fiction pushing in through his nostrils, his eyes rolling back, the fiction taking control of him just like he'd intended. There had been only five on the bus, two men sitting together near the front, an old, well-dressed lady in the row directly behind the men, a businessman in a suit halfway down the aisle, and a younger woman toward the back. The woman looked the nicest and Eli hoped to have someone to speak to on the journey, so he took a seat in the row behind her. The woman had a bag of Burger King on the seat next to her and the smell wafted back toward Eli, who hadn't eaten all day. To break the ice with the woman Eli said, *You're killing me with that smell.* Eli had always received top marks for his oral aptitude in his English classes and he was sure he spoke the words clearly. But the woman turned around with a face as if she was horrified and said, *What did you just say to me?* Eli said, *No, I just mean that the Burger King smells so good, it's torture.* The girl just looked at Eli a long time and then said, *I really don't understand what you're saying.* Eli gave up and felt immediately lonely. And then right at the last second, just before the bus was set to depart, a man got on, around forty, tall and muscular, with a shaved head. Nearly good looking. The man walked down the aisle, seeming to consider each seat, occupied or not, until he reached Eli who he stared at for a long second. Then he sat in the seat across the aisle from Eli.

Whenever you tell this, I imagine this guy as enormous. Like a god.

He was one of the biggest men I'd ever seen.

Ever?

Ever.

The bus pulled out of Victoria's dingy bus terminal and worked its way south, out of the city. The roads became rural and as they did, the man reached across the aisle to get Eli's attention. Eli turned to look at the man, who smiled at him, the creases in his forehead rippling over the whole of his bald head. He began asking questions which Eli deemed normal, where Eli was from, what Eli was doing in England, why Eli was going to Dover. Eli was happy for the conversation and he told the man he was going to hike the cliffs, that he'd heard they were sad and beautiful in a poem he'd had to study in school, that he wanted to see if the poem was true or false. Eli remembered it clearly, the look on the man's face when Eli said *sad and beautiful*, how the man cringed then looked back at Eli with a terrifying smile.

What do you mean he cringed?

Like he shivered. Or like, he recoiled.

And then smiled? Creepy.

Very creepy.

Très glauque.

Right?

Eli asked the man what he was doing on the bus and the man said he was going to Canterbury to see his mother. When Eli asked about the man's mother, the man seemed to grow agitated quickly and he cut Eli off with a muddled explanation that his mother was sick. Eli understood and didn't prod and the man asked why Eli was traveling. Not in the administrative sense, which Eli had already explained, but in the existential sense. Why with a capital *W*. What was Eli trying to understand? Eli hadn't considered any bigger reason than literary pleasure. The idea had struck him to travel, he loved the idea of England generally, and so he went, simple as that. But rather than give a boring answer such as, no real reason, which was the truth, Eli said something along the lines of, *To commune with the lies of my own reality and to bring them in line with the truths of my own imagination*. Bullshit, Eli thought, the moment he said it. Pretty bullshit that Eli realized very quickly was the wrong thing to have said. The man immediately began to fidget, looking hard at Eli while stroking his own face, seemingly having lost awareness of his actions. He looked at Eli in a way that Eli struggled to explain to his friends, as if the man was trying to force his soul into Eli's body. Then the man began to explain how he'd just returned to England from a three-year Christian mission he'd been on in Africa, namely for the sake of performing conversions. Eli asked what sort of conversions, but the man seemed not to hear him. The man went on, describing the moment in Africa when he'd been born again, how his life was now in the service of God. Then the man spoke a line that struck Eli, about how the man was in a perpetual state of repentance. But he didn't say what for. Eli wanted the conversation to end and for a long moment it did, the two sitting in silence and small music from the young woman's headphones filling the space. The man looked off out the window at the nondescript hills and, without looking at Eli, asked Eli if he was a Christian.

Yikes.

What are you even?

Jewish and Catholic, technically. But nothing, obviously. I was young. I didn't know what to say. I found any answer confusing.

Eli took a long time in answering the man. And the longer he took, it seemed to Eli that more and more the man wanted Eli to say he wasn't Christian. So he did. Eli said he wasn't a Christian.

Bizarre.

As in, he wanted to convert you?

I have no idea.

Around this moment, Eli's bus was pulling into Canterbury, the bus stop a parking lot with a bank of toilets and a view up the hill on the spires of the famous cathedral. Eli said a prayer, a thanks to whatever god had decided the man would be getting off the bus. Eli wondered if the archbishop could hear him thinking.

No, you forgot the part about the BAFTAs.

Shit. The BAFTA part.

In the moments before the bus pulled into Canterbury, it became clear to Eli that the man was trying to impress him, like many men had throughout Eli's life, impressings Eli had never followed. First, the man asked Eli if he knew what the BAFTAs were and when Eli said he didn't, the man said, they're like the Oscars but for England. The man told Eli the BAFTAs were that night. When Eli showed little interest, the man said he was friends with a famous film director who was up for an award. The man simply said *famous director* but he did not name them. Then the man told Eli that, actually, the friend had got the man tickets and he was himself going to the BAFTAs that night and that the ceremony would be *star studded*. He started listing off names like Benedict Cumberbatch and Tom Hiddleston and Tom Hardy, especially Tom Hardy, and implying that, if Eli was interested, the man could get him into the show and introduce him to them.

Eli, still trying to stay calm, attempted to understand how it was that, with it being five p.m. and the two of them riding a budget bus to Canterbury, the man could possibly have the time to see his mother and make it back to London, let alone have the personal connections to do so. It was chronologically impossible and Eli reprimanded himself for even attempting to understand it. The man didn't even have a duffle bag, let alone a tuxedo. He was only carrying a small backpack. Eli collected himself and said, that's really cool, I hope you have a good time. The response seemed to make the man even more nervous and he began breathing hard, nearly hyperventilating, Eli thought. The man could no longer hold eye contact with Eli and when Eli would look at him, the man would quickly avert his gaze.

Did you think about moving seats?

At this point I just figured he'd be off the bus soon.

He didn't get off the bus?

Don't ruin it.

So, the bus pulled into Canterbury and Eli started to relax. The five others on the bus, save the man and Eli, quickly got off and Eli watched them snake in various directions. Eli looked out the window and breathed, all while keeping a peripheral eye on the man. Eli liked the idea of having a bus all to himself, like he was on tour, like he was a star. The man was all the while rearranging his things, opening and closing his backpack, and Eli assumed the man was just taking his time. But then the bus driver climbed back on the bus and announced, *Taking off in five minutes. Everyone still on is going to Dover, yeah?* Eli looked at the man, his voice just beginning to falter, and said, *You're going to miss your stop.* The man looked calmly at Eli, grinning, and said, *Actually, I like your idea, about seeing the cliffs. I think I'll come to Dover with you.*

Non!

Yes.

Non, mais mec! C'est pas possible.

He said it as if he'd just graced me. Or saved me.

Mais, what the fuck?

Seriously, what the fuck, right?

Eli began to panic and without thinking, he picked up his bag and walked quickly down the aisle, toward the bus door. The man called to Eli, asking him where he was going. Compelled to a politeness that Eli himself couldn't understand, he turned to the man and said, *I'm going to have a look at the cathedral, actually*. Eli stepped down out of the bus and heard the man call after him, *Hold on, I'll come too then.* The panic became more lucid, more controllable, and the politeness fell away. Eli ducked behind another bus parked next to his, kept his head down, and found an angle from where he could watch the bus door. The man got off and looked around, nearly crazed. The man scanned for Eli and when he couldn't see him, the man nearly sprinted for the toilets. Eli reasoned that, upon losing Eli, the man would go looking for him in the cathedral. Remaining low in a crouch, a move Eli couldn't believe he was performing, something like Tom Cruise or Jason Bourne, Eli retraced his steps and snuck back onto the bus to Dover, much to the judgment of the driver, who looked at Eli like Eli was a lunatic. Skeptically, the driver turned over his shoulder and asked, *Ready to go?* Breathing relieved, Eli said, *Yeah, let's get out of here*. The driver closed the door, backed the bus out of its parking space and pulled toward the road. And just as the driver was waiting for a moment to pull out there came a violent banging on the bus, first on its rear quarter panel, then on its door.

Eli raised his eyebrows at his friends, in Paris, in the present.

Non. Non. Non. Non?

Oui.

The bus driver opened the door and Eli slid down in his seat. He heard the driver say, *We thought you'd snuck off,* to which the man said calmly, *I could say the same about you.*

Why didn't you just get off?

I was frozen. At that point I couldn't move.

The bus pulled away and Eli began to collapse inside himself. He could tell the man understood that the reality had shifted between them. That Eli had tried to lose him. But the man persisted and with a sharper voice now, tried to return the conversation to small talk. The man asked Eli what time Eli was going to see the cliffs and Eli told him not until the next day. Eli, wanting to shake the man loose from whatever he was concocting in his head, asked, *What about the BAFTAs?* He wanted the man to feel like he needed to go back to London. Eli could see that his question hurt the man for bringing reality to his attention. The man responded that he would see the cliffs, then head back. Eli looked at his phone. It was five thirty. Then Eli looked outside and it was starting to get dark. The man watched Eli judging his answers against the setting sun and again, reality shook the man. This time, Eli watched the reality change him. The man asked where Eli was planning to stay. If Eli knew people in Dover. Eli lied, saying he was staying with a friend he knew from university whose parents lived in Dover. For a moment, Eli was proud of himself for the lie. It sounded true and he'd spoken the lines naturally. The man's eyes lit up when Eli said it and he asked Eli if there might be a place for him to stay there too. Eli said no, that he didn't know the family very well. The answer clearly made the man angry. He broke eye contact with Eli for the first time and then said, *You could at least ask them, couldn't you?*

Don't forget about the snow.

Neither Léa nor Sarah liked the disco music Karim was playing over the bar's crackly speakers. It didn't go with Eli's story. The story needed slow bass. The story needed ominous techno, not floppy summer rhythms. Léa and Sarah made eye contact and agreed about the music, and by proxy about Eli. Eli was always talking about boys and girls, boyfriends and girlfriends. But he never had them. Not a single one in the six years Sarah and Léa had known him. Not in the history of Eli's love life recounted to them by Pierre, Rachel, and Marie. Eli was a natural flirt who was good at practice but bad at the actual act. With his friends he could be romantic. With the public, he was always more comedian than potential mate. Léa and Sarah hurt, for him, for that. The fact that Eli could craft narratives of passion in precedence, in theory, but when set face to face he always made friends. Just friends. Eli was gorgeous, in his way. Thick-bodied and Slavic. Compassionate and attentive. Except, something had ruined him, in love. Léa and Sarah had guessed at and discussed it once a week, or once a month, depending on the season. They'd tried to give him subtle advice, which Eli always recognized and got defensive against. Eli was a broken machine when it came to his lusting, broken in the way that no new parts could correct the problem. Léa and Sarah had been spending more time together. When Sarah had to come into Paris, she would often stop to check Léa and the baby. And Léa had twice come out to the house, so the baby could play in a garden. Léa and Sarah would start their discussions with Jude and Pierre, how they might be able to get them back together, a topic that quickly soured in their mouths and led them to drinking wine and changing the subject, often to Eli. And much wine had been sloshed over and wasted on discussing Eli's problem. Bottles of wine Léa and Sarah had drunk for tinkering, thumbs almost literally in the waistbands of their mechanic minds, perpetually the newest additions to the group and so tasked with its fiddling, assessing problems until the stakes of the problems became irrelevant and the mystery of the problems became entertainment, and so Léa and Sarah were just drinking to drink and avoiding a true answer or logical solution.

Thirty minutes from the scheduled arrival in Dover,

the situation took an even more ridiculous turn. The man asked if Eli knew what part of Dover Eli's friend lived in, if the friend planned to pick Eli up from the bus stop, that it would be nighttime by the time they arrived and that it might be dangerous for Eli, if he didn't know where he was going. It was like in the movies, Eli thought, because when the man said *dangerous*, all of a sudden the sky grew dark, with a black cloud blocking out the last of the daylight. And from the cloud began a torrential dumping of snow.

You're kidding.

What year did you say this was again?

What are you doing, Matt? Put your phone away.

I just want to check if it was actually snowing in Dover.

Rachel and Marie thought together about danger and how much of it they'd been in, together and separately. Paris was a city of danger, just like the world is a city, full of back alleys and side streets and broken-doored entryways. A world of countries as neighborhoods, centuries of them, with danger in them, always, both hiding and walking around, riding the buses and Métro. Marie and Rachel knew the snowing feeling of danger coming. Of danger being inescapable and having to wait patiently for its arrival. Every time they'd heard Eli's story before, this part gave them sympathy. Hard sympathy and heavy breathing. Eli's snow made them feel violent, a stockpile of violence as befitting the quantity of danger. Rachel and Marie could remember the phone calls to one another, in the early mornings, each saying, *Can I come over*. The request not being a question. Each could remember pulling out of their sleep to listen to the other, slowly fuming but not surprised, sitting cross-legged on the end of their bed with their friend shaking, wrapped in their blanket, still wearing their clothes. Heat played a sick joke on danger, since danger required blankets and hot showers and countless turns of repeating phrases. Rachel and Marie could still feel grips on necks and fists on hips, the squeezing disgustingly similar to invited pleasure. They were aware of how their pleasure could so easily be ruined now, with the wrong sort of familiar touching. The night, now, was hot with freedom and the unaccomplished journey of their impending walk home. After Eli finished his story, it would soon be time for the bar to close. They would all go their separate ways. Rachel and Marie looked at one another and winked, Rachel with her left eye, Marie with her right. Their memories made them mirror. Their wink was recognition of a membership.

The bus slowed and Eli could hear the driver cursing at the snow. His fear grew and from it Eli grew quiet, trying to remain silent to contain it. But the man questioned: What would Eli do for dinner? What would Eli do the next day? What would Eli do if his friend didn't show up, because of the snow storm? It got to the point when Eli couldn't take it and he said to the man, *Look, I'm sorry, but I don't really feel like talking*. And that's when everything turned bad. Worse than Eli could have imagined. The man started fidgeting again, only this time, more violently. Like rocking in his seat and bowing, nearly prostrating. Then he started bouncing more and rubbing his head with his knuckles, *like a fucking lunatic,* Eli thought. Then the man pulled out the small laminated brochure for the bus line services from the pouch attached to the seat in front of him and he flipped through it, over and over, but not slow enough to read it. Then he put the brochure away. Then took it back out again. Flipped it again. And again. And the slapping noise of the brochure flipping took on a horrific rhythm in Eli's mind and Eli closed his eyes so he wouldn't have to see the man. But he could still hear the brochure slapping. As the man repeated the routine again and again, Eli came to understand that something bad was about to happen. Eli walked to the front of the moving bus. He caught the driver's eye in the rearview mirror and the driver yelled at Eli to sit down. Eli sat and asked the driver if there were any more buses going back to London that night. As if the question oppressed him, the driver said there was one more return scheduled, but there was no way it would run in this snow.

The last time you told it, the guy wasn't rubbing his head and jerking all around.

Would you shut up, Matt? Jesus.

I would have fucked that guy up.

No you wouldn't have, Jude.

Yes I would have. You've got to shut that kind of shit down before it starts.

Pierre and Jude nodded at one another like they both would have fucked that guy up. That they would have shut that shit down. You had to. You had to show you were not to be fucked with. That you were not to be made property of someone else's perversions. They could say so because they knew what was coming. They'd heard the story before so they knew nothing bad happened. But they knew how close Eli had come. And they knew that in the long leadup to nothing, when everything terrible was still possible, a fear had been born in Eli that he continued to hold onto now. Pierre and Jude felt their muscles tense under their clothes because they knew the fear and they could feel it in places much farther down than their muscles. Pierre could feel the pair of strong hands on his biceps, another pair of hands holding him by his neck against the vestibule wall, a third pair taking his phone out of his pocket, demanding his code, then all the hands relaxing when he finally gave it. Pierre could feel the strain of his eyes as he tried not to blink, watching the hands for knives as the young muggers, no older than eighteen, just boys, tried to decide what to do next. Pierre could sense their desperation and it worried him more than if they knew better what they were doing. One of the teens asked if Pierre had any money and Pierre instinctively said no, though later he realized he did, nearly one hundred euros. The muggers didn't search him, and the fact that they could have made Pierre strain in the future at the idea of what would have happened if they had. Pierre felt the pose of the ball he'd rolled into immediately after the boys had left. And he remembered the sour taste of his mouth as he hard-swallowed before entering the party, pretending like nothing had happened. At the same time, Jude felt the arch of his back, and the hard body behind it. The rough and cracked hand on his chin and the dull knife on his throat. The pressure of it cleaving him open. Jude could still hear the sound he'd made when he realized what was happening, in his own vestibule, so close to the safety of his home. A pitiful squeal, Jude made. And Jude could still feel the physical confusion he'd felt, triggered by a demand in a foreign language, a demand he'd struggled to translate, that he give over *all his bitch money.* Jude's pockets had only twenty euros of bitch money and as he handed it over, Jude wondered what it cost to avoid a throat-cutting. He was sure it was more than twenty euros. Jude heard the man behind him, his lips against Jude's ear, in the past, saying *Whore, son of a whore,* then taking the blade off Jude's jugular. Jude tried not to remember the shame he'd felt when getting into bed, shivering and somehow hard. Then the touching he'd done for a reason he still couldn't explain to himself. Jude looked at Pierre and thought about the story Pierre had told him, about getting mugged, and how for some reason it made him hate Pierre even more. For how much of the life Jude wanted, Pierre had already accomplished. Even the horrors. Jude hadn't told Pierre about his own assault. And so when Pierre nodded back at Jude a second time, and he saw Jude's jaw clenching just like his, firm, not to be fucked with, Pierre thought he and Jude were in agreement, when actually the two men didn't recognize one another at all.

This next part is crazy.

I love this next part.

The bus pulled in to its stop at Dover, a stretch of

pavement only slightly wider than the sidewalk in what looked to Eli like the suburbs of a rural village. There was no station, and as such, no fellow travelers there waiting. There to keep Eli company. The man had finally fallen silent in his seat. He was no longer rocking or flipping, but when Eli glanced at him, he could see he was shaking, almost vibrating, and then he crossed himself violently. Eli stood to get off the bus and he could feel the man stand and follow close behind him, no more than a few inches. Eli was at a loss for what to do. The sky was dark, in its last phase of gray before night, and Eli could see no open shops or restaurants. Stepping down from the bus, Eli looked at the driver who nodded to Eli in a way that confused him. As if he understood. For at that moment, fate stepped in, or maybe providence, and as Eli struggled to decide between turning left or right he heard the driver clear his throat and say to the man, *Alright sir, you're coming with me.* Like a policeman.

Or an angel.

Or an angel.

The man was taken aback and the driver reminded him that he hadn't yet paid for his ticket to Dover. That he owed the driver for the second leg of the trip. The man said he didn't have any cash. Feeling caught in a miracle, Eli lingered to witness. The driver explained to the man that the nearest cash point was a few blocks away and that the driver would escort the man to it. Clearly shaken, the man turned to look back at Eli, still frozen. Eli could tell the man was confused, his brain stuck between running from and chasing. Finally, Eli felt the more practical half of his brain, left or right, Eli wasn't sure, forcing him to move and he clipped the straps of his traveler's backpack. He turned in the opposite direction of the man and began to sprint, his instinct taking him into a nondescript residential housing estate. Without so much as a thought, or a hand to leverage him, Eli hopped the fence around one of the first houses he came to and hid in the yard. He checked his phone but his phone was dead, not that he knew the number for Emergency in England. Eli sat there for nearly two hours, waiting, the snow falling and building up in the yard, Eli protected by a wall of winter rose bushes. And when no one came for him, Eli stood, unlatched the garden's gate and walked toward the center of town where he knew his hotel was. Somewhere.

You just sat there? No one saw you?

No one.

Putain. And you didn't see the guy again? He didn't find you?

He didn't find me.

Bullshit.

What?

Bullshit.

Matt, shut up. Let him tell it.

This story always changes. Sometimes there's the BAFTAs. Sometimes there's snow. It seems made up to me. Like Eli is riffing on some *King Lear* LARP. The story is too perfect.

By the February in question, Gretchen had been living

in Dover for twenty years by herself and herself alone. Her first two decades could be viewed as a single evening, the militant routine of her days collapsing the decades into a single, smooth mean. The day was decades of solace and peace. Exactly what Gretchen needed. Peace had been easy in the daylight and so the days in Dover were easy, though tiring. Tiring because the solace left her sitting up nights beside her picture window, the weight of the dark pressing in against the glass and Gretchen's forehead pressing back against the glass's insides. After that night in February, however, a silent night Gretchen could not explain, the dark of the coming years came to be defined by a single image, one that did not haunt Gretchen but did persist and as such drew its own smooth average through Gretchen's future solitude.

Outside the glass there were always the roses bushes, winter blooming, including when she'd bought the terraced house, and of which Gretchen became the caretaker. Under Gretchen's astute supervision the bushes had flourished and now they ran longways across the garden's low stone wall. In winter the roses waited, open, and Gretchen, herself opening, waited with them. Gretchen's garden clippers also waited, balanced on their tips beside the door, waiting for Gretchen to decide what should be cut out so that the plants might survive for another blossom.

Sometimes, in the night garden, in the solace, there were foxes and the foxes stopped Gretchen's aging heart. Usually they were alone, just like her, slinking and planning and resting. For that she felt sympathy. When the foxes were alone, Gretchen named them because they seemed peaceful, friendly. But the few times foxes were together, when there were multiple foxes, she didn't name anyone. Not from lack of desire but because foxes together were criminals. They disturbed the peace. They fought and dominated. They made scenes that Gretchen hated and couldn't look away from. Eventually, one or the other would always let out a scream, thankfully dulled by the window's double pane.

On the night in question, February 2011, two men entered her garden like foxes. First one, panting. Then another, clearly chasing. The second, so much larger, so much smoother than the first. In her garden they fought, first silently, sweat breaking out on the bigger man's head. Both fought, but the bigger one dominated. The bigger fox, as always. Gretchen watched and said nothing. She didn't intervene or name the men. She watched and waited for the screaming, which finally came like it always did. Gretchen never told anyone. Gretchen had no one to tell.

What do you mean too perfect?

Black clouds. Divine intervention. Two hours in a blizzard. It's bullshit.

So what if it is? Do you have a better story to tell?

Piss off.

I didn't think so.

You can be a real piece, you know that Matt?

Sometimes there was snow and sometimes there wasn't. Sometimes there were BAFTAs and sometimes there weren't. Sometimes the bus drove fast and sometimes it drove slowly and sometimes it skidded in the snow but regardless of speed Eli's story always ended perfectly. Matt found the story so anticlimactic. It had the most exciting escape. It left everyone who heard the story to assume the danger, which was the perfect way to craft a villain. But who knew what the nervous Christian with the big arms and hard body was thinking? His nerves could have so easily been misinterpreted. Eli's hiding played to audience desire, for him to have outwitted and outplayed an oppressor. And it presumed guilt. And it biased them. Every time Matt heard the story, it got more exciting, the build got better and the setting more ominous. But the better the telling, the more disappointing the ending. And the more Matt wished something bad had actually happened. Matt looked around at the bodies of his friends, all slouching, all starting to sag. Matt could see the first dashes of gray above Pierre's ears and Léa's temples. He could see Rachel struggling to relieve a kink in her neck. He felt the doughy weakness at the table and his ability to have his way with anyone around it, save maybe Eli. Matt thought of push-ups and he thought of dips and he thought of the men he saw cleaving themselves around the public workout equipment near his apartment. He thought of what his muscles were worth, as they rotted. Matt nearly dropped down to the ground to relieve himself with push-ups, like his doctor had said might be good for him. But Matt took two deep breaths and collected himself.

Fine Matt, it didn't happen like that. Does that make

you feel better?

It does actually.

Ta mère, Matthieu. Enculé.

Eli thought about the fiction in his story. He wished the parts untold didn't make the story more fictional in their absence. Eli didn't like being a documentary. He didn't like having a story in his history that made him worth a cheap and cringy series. And though he enjoyed the attention in the act of telling, Eli hated the inquiries that came from the story's telling. He feared the repetition. The idea that one time he would slip up in recounting and reveal. That Eli might include a new and improvised sentence that gave away a truth he'd been careful in masking. Eli thought about the girl in the beginning, eating her Burger King and not understanding what he was saying. She was the kindest, in her cold way. And sometimes Eli wished that everyone was like her, incapable of comprehending his words, turning away from him in disgust when he spoke.

You've got to finish the story.

I'm done.

Just tell it. Forget Matt, he's just being a bitch.

You can't stop there. You're leaving off the best part.

There's more?

Yeah, it gets crazier.

No really, I'm done.

I'll tell it then. So Eli leaves the yard and goes to where he's supposed to be staying, which was like, this creepy bar with an inn above it, right?

Yeah.

And when Eli walks in, it's like a scene out of a movie. Everyone in the pub goes silent and turns to look at him. There's a guy behind the bar who goes, *Elijah? We've been waiting for you.* Or some creepy shit like that. They check him in and take him up to his room. And the room is terrible. Eight bunk beds, or something, all with used sheets still on them. And the guy goes, *Oh sorry, I must have forgotten to do the cleaning.* Eli says he doesn't care, he just wants to know if it's the only room available. As in, if someone else shows up, would they be in the room with him? Because he's worried the guy from the bus will show up and be put in his room too. And the guy says, *Yeah, this is the only room. Why?*

So then Eli is left in the room, alone, freaking out. And he sits there for an hour trying to figure out what to do. He looks up if there's any way to get back to London and he can't find any. The only option would be to take a cab, for like, 400 pounds. And the whole time he's just waiting for the door to open. For the guy to walk in and for Eli to be trapped in the room with him. So he sits there, basically having a panic attack, and he pushes a few of the bunk beds in front of the door, just to buy him some time, you know? But then he decides, fuck it, I have to go down to the bar and face the situation and try to make friends with the guy running the pub, in case the guy from the bus does show up.

Yeah, he goes down to the pub and starts schmoozing with everyone. Being all Eli. There's what, the bartender and two old guys, and like, one of their wives, and another old woman?

And there's the Irish guy who's speaking gibberish, who everyone can understand except Eli.

Yeah, what was his name?

Mick.

Yeah Mick!

I love this part.

Didn't he say something to you, and everyone cracked up and said like, good one Mick? And you had no idea what he'd said?

So they're all having a good time, drinking, playing pool, having Eli try all this weird English pub food. What was it they had you try?

Pickled eggs.

Gross. Yeah, so they're getting drunk, and telling Eli stories about their life in Dover. How one of the guys there, the one there with his wife, is like, the tough guy in town. They call him Killer Bill, or Killer Brian, or something. But he's actually super nice and his wife's being all sweet and motherly to Eli too. Killer Bill's wife. And Eli is starting to feel good because he knows they'll be on his side if the guy from the bus shows up.

So it's getting late and everyone says it's time for them to head home. But then they open the door, and there's what, like a foot of snow piled up against the door? And they all try to get their cars out and drive home, but they can't, because the roads are bad and they can't even make it up the hill just outside the pub.

Everyone comes back inside and they keep drinking and Eli's relaxed. They get the fire going big and bring out nice whiskey and are saying that it's really nice to meet him. That Eli's a good egg. *A good pickled egg*, Killer Bill's wife says.

And then the guy running the pub stands up and walks to the door, and Eli thinks he's just going to open it and check on the snow but instead he locks the door from the inside and turns around and says, alright Elijah, this has been nice, but now you have a decision to make.

What?

Yeah!

Eli, you tell it. You tell it so well.

No.

Eli, tell it.

Fine.

The man running the pub had an odd look on his face. One of perversion, as he waited for Eli to answer. Eli was drunk, and the question spun in his head as he failed to understand himself taking an active role in the experience. Eli stared for a moment into the burning coals of the stove the group now sat around. Veins of heat crackled and snaked around the coals. Eli looked back at the pub owner, then at the rest of the patrons who were each watching him. The manager cleared his throat and said, *Your decision is, you can either say nice to meet us and go up to bed now. Or, you can stay and listen. But if you stay and listen and ever tell anyone what you've heard, we'll fucking kill you.*

And? *Tu as fais quoi?*

I stayed, obviously.

Thank God!

The group sitting around the fire began discussing a man who had wronged them. Someone who had got in the way of their business. One who needed to be taught a lesson. One of the group explained his morning routine, how he always drove the same road at the same time. Another explained the road. Where they could lay in wait.

Were they planning on killing him?

The men spoke about needing the *tools*. Asking who had the *tools*. Who would do what with which *tools*. And where the women would put the *tools* when they were done with them. Then they discussed who would drive the cars. Where they would meet up after. And then, fast as it had become nefarious, it turned wholesome. The manager looked at the group and said, *Alright everyone, we really should get some sleep so we're fresh for this in the morning*. The group stood, all except the bartender and Mick. They said their goodbyes and shuffled out of the pub. No one seemed to worry about the snow. The manager walked Eli to his room, patted him on the back and said goodnight. His nerves shot, Eli pushed the bunk beds back in front of the door. He repacked his backpack, put his jacket and boots back on, and only then did he lie down in one of the beds blocking the door. To give it extra weight, Eli decided. Eli closed his eyes and tried to perform breathing exercises in the hopes that maybe he might sleep. But after ten minutes of trying he was shaken out of his forced meditation by a faint but repeating sound. Eli sat up to listen. Through the walls he could clearly make out the sound of a pickax strike and then the sound of a shovel digging.

Come on.

Seriously. Digging.

No.

What other sound could it have been? It was digging.

They were messing with you. You're not making this up?

I'm not making this up.

They were messing with you. They had to have been.

Yeah, they probably were.

And? So?

The digging lasted for over an hour. Eli sat upright, his back to the door, fading in and out of hallucinations. Sometimes he was more than half asleep and in those moments he lived the man pushing in on the door, the bunk beds tipping like dominoes. At five in the morning, Eli could take the situation no longer. He got out of bed, silently moved the bunks aside, and descended the stairs. A faint glow still smoldered in the stove, but Eli found himself alone. He tested the front door and it was locked, but there was no key. Eli could feel a draft coming from near the staircase and he followed it, finding a hallway that led to a back door that led to an open courtyard. As he left he tried to make out the space, to see if there was a hole, but it was still too dark to see.

Did you even go to see the cliffs?

Eli followed the town signage pointing to the cliffs. The cold wind buffeting the high beach grasses that carried him upward. The walk was long and Eli froze in it as the path carried him higher. After forty-five minutes, the path finally crested, dipped, and crested again, then turned left onto an outcropping, beyond which exploded the white of the cliffs. From the lookout, Eli could see the cliffs stretching miles in front of him and a path that would take him along them. Eli waited as the first full light of the morning diffused into the scene. About a thirty-minute walk ahead of him, Eli estimated, he could see what looked like a figure standing at the edge of the cliffs where the green of the turf met the white of the wall's chalk face. A lighthouse turned behind in the sunrise. The figure moved slightly and Eli struggled to make it out. He wondered if it was just a shadow play from the lighthouse's spinning beam. He blinked, and the figure was gone. Eli imagined the man jumping from the rocks and the idea cut against the cold of the wind. He blinked again and the figure had returned. Eli recited Shakespeare in his head:

methought his eyes
Were two full moons; he had a thousand noses,
Horns whelked and waved like the enragèd sea.
It was some fiend. Therefore, thou happy father,
Think that the clearest gods, who make them honors
Of men's impossibilities, have preserved thee.

And then Eli chastised himself. He turned back, not having reached the cliffs, technically, but having seen them. In the town center there was only one cafe open and Eli entered. A kind old woman looked at him and furrowed her brow. Eli asked if she knew when the first bus was scheduled back to London. The woman took a long time to answer, then said, *Half an hour*. Eli lingered and the woman asked if he'd like some food while he waited. Eli looked at the menu and couldn't understand it. The woman said, *Get the full English. Looks like you could use it darling*. In no time at all, a steaming plate of bacon and sausage and shaved potato triangles was placed in front of Eli and he inhaled it.

You've never told this part before.

Haven't I?

You don't eat meat?

I know.

Eli didn't eat meat, but at that moment he felt like he deserved it. Not even, that he needed the meat for the sake of his health. The woman said, *Sweetie, it doesn't look like you slept a wink last night*, as she refilled his milky tea. Eli didn't know how to explain, so he only said she was right, that he hadn't, but that the breakfast was helping. He told her it was his first English breakfast. The woman smiled at him and so Eli tipped her, more than the price of the food, and then he left and got on the bus back to London. Eli remembered the flavor of the breakfast in his mouth. He didn't feel guilty for eating the meat, not then and not now, because the meat had made him sick on the bus ride back.

The sky above the roundabout had, that evening, gone from blue to blue-pink to yellow to orange to red to pink-blue then to violet. Eli caught the sky at its violet as he stepped out to smoke his cigarette. The spotlights were switched on and began to rotate through the sky. Failing to calm, Eli smoked another cigarette as the violet became indigo. When the night was finally black, an odd silence swept over the neighborhood like the wind had been knocked out of it. It wasn't like a summer evening to go so quiet, up high above the city where the sounds of revelers carried. Eli waited. Finally calmed himself. Then from Rue des Cascades came a pack of children, running, screaming, shortly followed by a pack of bigger children, Roman candles in their hands, the small mortars shooting horizontally at the fleeing targets. The crackers popped into hundreds of burning cherries which bounced off the cobbles and ricocheted blindly into the full limbs of the tree. For a moment the roundabout was lit like a sinners' festival and the waves of sound and light broke against Eli's body as the children ran past him up Rue des Envierges. The scene quieted for a moment. Eli lit another cigarette. Then the back suck of the wave built and the pursuers had turned to prey. The attackers flew backward toward Cascades, the empty firework casings still in their hands as even larger children countercharged with their own Roman candles popping off. Eli caught faces, frozen in the strobing explosions, the light making eye bags and drooping jowls, boys' and girls' faces who looked like they'd been beyond their years long before their birth. Children whose youth was hand-me-down from those who'd never had the chance to use it. Immaturity from some other age, from some other epoch, youth who had been lined up against a wall and asked for final words.

One of our other friends got mugged two blocks from home, two nights in a row. Same place, both times. The exact same staircase. Nearly the exact same step. On the second mugging, our friend had nothing left to mug. The stairs looked dangerous, but they weren't. Weren't, we agreed, until the strikes changed everything about nights. Made everything nice about nights into danger. Beautiful, mutual danger. We walked the long distances home, learning new shortcuts because there were no night buses or Métro. The nights were a beauty with people. People out in winter outfits, walking and wishing for safer transport, night buses that were never coming. Walking and waiting to wish, then walking on again, when they'd built up the courage. We walked and we saw couples and groups standing still, waiting out the cold for better options, inviting one another to stay over, saying they really shouldn't, saying they should really get home, then relenting, agreeing, out of fear, in relief. We saw bars struggling to close, their bartenders nervous about their own journeys home, everyone lingering, working up to giving in. We agreed, one night, finally, to sleep together. So we could all feel safe getting home. We were walking when another group got to walking behind us. We didn't believe it to be following. We didn't feel nervous. We were all in groups. And we were together. And we just hoped that they felt safe around us, no worse than us to them. At a quiet place, in a shortcut that would get us home quicker, the other group got closer. One of theirs slipped a hand in the pocket of one of ours, sort of like a handshake. We were at a loss for words. We could not remember our names. All we could think about was screaming.

And that was all we did. They screamed back, startled at our reaction. Then we all got quiet and looked at one another and both of us, all of us, looked extremely beautiful.

Matt and Marie get back together

A Friday on the roundabout, its population mounting, bodies filling the traffic circle from the outside inward. The sidewalks becoming full and then people having to stand in the road. The cars slowing, muted drivers waving in their silent cabs, begging to be released from the scene. The spotlights of the Eiffel turning around in the sky, inescapable. The sound of hellos beating faster, smokers lighting cigarettes, giving cigarettes to strangers, to anyone asking. Everyone smiling, some stepping in the road to hug, to kiss, to be reminded of part-time love, weekend love, love with a beer in hand. The roundabout beginning to roll. Beginning to collapse in on itself. Friends stepping back into bars, more friends exiting bars, friends pushing toward the beech tree, searching for relief, for space to say hello to new arrivals, space to be introduced to new best friends, old best friends they never speak to. Space to smoke. Friendships being pushed to the limits, escaping slightly down the side roads, finding room for discretion, places to be lifted up, to say hello without being seen.

The drugs knew Rachel, Matt, Jude, and Léa. Marie, Eli, Pierre, and Sarah. Rach, Matthieu, Judas, and Lee, Mary, E, Pete, and Sally. Rachel Justine and Matthew Blake. Jude Butler and Léa Christine. Marie Séverine and Elijah Abraham. Pierre Paolo and Sarah Claude. All eight. They all knew the drugs. But they hadn't seen each other in years. The drugs were doing well. The drugs were doing fine. The drugs were good. The drugs were good to run into again. The drugs were taller, maybe? Or, stronger? Had the drugs been working out? But then, there was something different about the drugs. Their energy. Their tone. Were the drugs judging? Were the drugs looking down at them? The drugs like drones, lifting? The drugs like new arguments, interrupting? Misinterpreting?

Jesus, these are strong.

Mmm.

Putain.

Where'd you get them from?

Off some guy I know.

Quel guy?

Some guy.

I didn't know you still knew a guy.

Just in case. You know.

For these uncertain times?

Précisément.

When's the last time we did this?

Ça fait longtemps, non?

A while.

Why do they have these little ghosts on them?

Because they're supposed to be good.

You probably shouldn't snort them.

But I want to. Like we used to.

It's going to hurt.

Non, ça va être bon.

Très bon.

God, I can already feel them.

Wasn't the last time that party out in Clichy?

Like, four years ago?

Oh yeah! Remember Eli?

Remember Rachel, you mean.

Was that the time Marie and Matt...?

No.

Shit.

Careful.

Quoi?

You just spilled like a pill's worth.

Don't exaggerate. That's just a key.

Chill.

The dust worked its way into the capillaries of the asphalt and with winter moisture it dissolved quickly.

Drugs so strong they control the dialogue?

No.

Drugs so good they begin to narrate?

No.

Drugs so bad they raise the dead?

No.

Drugs so pure they free the scene?

Maybe.

The roundabout spun back on itself, clockwise, against traffic. An old Lada honked and pumped its brakes. The roundabout's eyes rolled back and it could feel the beech tree's dormant seeds. To the east, the yellow moon of winter, but only winking. And on the ground the yellow moonlight licked. The light warmed white and reddish cells, the crescent shape of moons, slicing quickly through pulsing arteries, down only one-way roads. Directions spilled from out its nose, leaking, accelerating, merging onto streets and highways. In the moon heat, the reds left behind with whites inside turned quickly brown, dried, then let the gutters take them. And in the gutters, now running clean, a needle here and a dented canister. Pleasures eddying the flow.

Why don't we do this more often?

You're one to ask.

What does that mean?

Nothing.

What's everyone think about this shit?

What shit?

This shit everyone's talking about.

Give us a break man.

Don't talk about it.

Remember the time we found Jude all the way down in front of the cathedral? What were you debating that guy about?

Laïcité.

Of course. Always *laïcité.*

How did you get all the way down there?

You were fucked.

He did win the debate. That's for sure.

In the sharp air of a cold midwinter, the scented sounds of the city bloomed. A scooter ripped the night with diesel, and where its wheels kissed the flowing gutter concrete blood and motion rose. Road sent moonward, gaseous now, toward desperate, huffing lungs. An air of pleasure to be passed around. The scent, strong in the nostrils, of boy groups and girls strutting for one another, incapable of anything but to snort and exhale. Jaws grinding and heels grinding and the last strands of street cut freer. The first fears of freedom. The paranoia. The security of other smokers, politeness holding doors that frame the sidewalks, foundations making subtle claims of guilt, scolding the evaporating street and pushing it onward.

Qui a du feu?

Moi.

Meuf!

Quoi?

Tu es belle toi.

Shut up.

Non. Comme le disent les Américains. Tu es AH-may-zing?

Comment ça se passe avec Nathan?

Behave yourself.

Quoi?

He's right over there?

Ça va. Ça va faire un an, non?

More like six months.

Vraiment? Seulement six mois?

Yes.

Tu n'es pas encore défoncée?

Pas encore.

You want to take another?

The smell of the asphalt's pleasure collects over crowded terraces, where it's tugged up by their pulsing heaters, thrown down by waiting cold, taken into lips through cigarettes, then blown free to higher vistas. The vents of shuttered bakeries get their turn at it, stealing some of the pleasure to ferment and tint the pastries waiting for tomorrow's eating. Gas-brushed treats like advertisements, screaming. The night's fog body builds its odor, hoisting itself into windows above the bakery, the building windows fitted with debating parties. Arms and arguments of parties, spilling out of windows, hands flapping upward in disagreements over politics, fingers whipping and flicking the faulted pleasure a little higher, to better parties, where love is being discussed, one, two, three stories higher. A ladder of stories told and retold, until the inflated roundabout lands upon the roof. The clouds arrive for opportunity, make bravado and dramatic huffs, throw their gusts in a stinging churning, freeing the built environment into the night. And so, this total convection of our pleasure, chemicals converted into more refreshing states, an air of rocks and evolutions. Inklings of things to come. Of things to be. Of things forever bound for our atmosphere.

How many did you take?

One and a half.

Slow down big man. It's only eleven thirty.

Who do you think you are, giving me advice?

Basically your brother, at this point.

Well then I distinctly remember my brother tweaking, thinking he was having a heart attack last time we did these together.

My point exactly.

But your heart attack was a panic attack.

Fuck you.

What?

I asked you not to tell anybody about that.

Sarah must know.

What are you two talking about?

Nothing.

Matt, you ready for another half?

Finally, free to crack its back, the roundabout reached out its arms into the small universe over lower Paris and felt its first true pleasure. The circle kneeled at the sight of what it was connected to, but above the traffic now. The moon grew quickly full at the sight of such pleasure kneeling, wriggling beneath it. Unable to bear it any longer, the roundabout stood and let itself become the breeze. A pleasure in the air.

I feel like we don't really see each other anymore.

We saw each other last week.

Not like that. You know what I mean.

What do you mean?

I don't know.

You know I love you.

Is that the drugs talking?

Probably.

Well, when you put it like that?

Stop. Things are just weird with work.

But you just got a promotion or something. Didn't you?

Yeah but it's confusing.

And Matt just told me you're buying an apartment.

Trying to.

Why didn't you tell me?

I don't know. The bank hasn't approved my loan, so nothing is certain.

But this is what I mean. Why did I have to hear it from Matt?

Because I don't know if I'll get approved.

Of course you'll get approved. You have a cigarette for me?

Always.

We're spending too much time with Jude and Matt. They've got us speaking English.

Putain. We're just high.

Yes we is.

Are.

Merde.

Putain de merde.

Tu parles encore à Maxime?

Jamais. Ne-ver.

C'est bien ça. If you ever do, that is something you can forget to tell me about.

Tais-toi.

Are you talking to anyone these days?

Pas du tout.

That can't be true.

Believe me.

The new breeze eyed itself between the needles of the Lebanese cedars that savage Buttes Chaumont. The pride-pleasure of being evergreen set the trees' parakeets to calling, making the birds greener and less foreign. Pleasure had put them there, on foreign soil, though clearly someone else's broken pleasure. And in the broken places the birds had fled their bounds and integrated the pleasure-test of northern winters, steadied in the public park. There's a certain pleasure made mythic by the glory of house pets devolving, escaping their faulted owners, thriving outside human care. The moonlight slapped the cocky smile off one of these parakeets. It squawked and puffed its breast. A young girl out shockingly past her bedtime noticed below, pointed, and began to screech. The girl recognized her sibling, her sister across species, green and hiding in the trees. The girl expressed her pleasure in the French, not the birdsong, and was shushed by her mother's foreign tongue. Scolded with older, more violent, indecipherable sentences, this daughter answered calmly. No, she was not an embarrassment. She simply had her mother's pride, but pride of a different place. The mother and her child. The terrifying pride of different self-recognition. The wet calm pride of pleasure that, though strong, cannot prevent our secret crying.

You okay babe?

I'm fine, yeah.

What's wrong?

Are we bad, for this?

For what?

Aren't we just a bit old for it?

He's fine. He's with your mother. She's great with him.

I know he's fine. I'm not talking about him.

You used to love this.

I still do. But isn't that the problem?

I don't know.

I know you said you needed this.

I never said that. I said I wanted it.

What is it you want?

The freedom, I guess.

From what?

Not from you babe. We've waited to do this until you were ready.

I know. Sorry.

Don't apologize.

Do you feel good?

Yeah. Do you?

Yeah.

Good.

Take another with me? One last time.

It would be my pleasure.

Can we sniff it?

Of course we can. Do you have a bill?

Yeah one second.

And still the wind continues, it spins the air with the pleasure in it. And still, our pleasure. The roundabout. Teasing. Blowing. Licking the earlobes of the smudged and smutty churches. Firming the architecture. Setting the streetlights a little straighter. Then fleeing to the other side of town, its newfound right. Above the gates of the Luxembourg Gardens hang the cold-dead arms of grand horse chestnuts, tree skeletons dead temporarily, like the heat-dead limbs of desert horses. The fear-pleasure of all opportunities occurring before our death. And the sounds that play when wind blows through them. Knocks them down. Underneath the nightshade of the branches stand a group of migrant workers, thick-fingered and dusty from labor, drinking their pleasure out of cans. They huddle together laughing and exaggerating, lying for a pleasure warmth to face the winter with. So much sex in a well-timed joke. So much opportunity for eye contact and a slap on the back. One of the men, of the boys, feels the fear-pleasure of whistling distance, the nearness of his favorite coworker's swollen shoulders and sweated neck. He bets on the nearsightedness of his other coworkers' searching eyes. He feels his arm lifting, senses the solitary arm wrestle of fear, of his arm flexed to searching, and of that same dead limb as it pinned itself in shame, the bravery too heavy. The bulk-toned fear of pleasure in saying it can wait, that patience, and the knowing that it really can't. That it never will.

Thanks for getting these.

Mmm.

You feeling good?

Mmm.

You can't still be mad.

Can't I?

It's a different year.

It's the same life.

Touché.

You speak French now?

Ta gueule.

Well done.

I said I'm sorry. I was drunk.

You're always drunk.

We have that in common.

Touché. I'm touched.

Nice.

Mmm.

What do you want me to do?

You could say you're sorry.

I have. Many times.

Not like that.

Fuck off.

That's more like it.

Are you fucking with me?

Always, baby love.

So you're not still mad.

I didn't say that.

Jesus.

Change the subject. You're boring me.

What do you want to talk about?

Mmm. How about you and Rachel?

Stop man. Don't fuck with me.

Odd. I could have sworn you were a bottom.

Mmm.

You sound more and more like me.

Mmm.

Don't be sensitive. Most goals are hotter left unaccomplished, *tu sais?*

A break in the wind so that we might really feel it picking back up again, blowing so, but from new directions. A pause so that pleasure might be granted the chance to please itself. The roundabout gets itself lost in the lonely extremities of the city, in Bois de Boulogne and Bois de Vincennes, caught in their rubber trees and endless sycamores. Too much oxygen. Too much breathing to clear the head. Not enough dirty city between its lungs to dumb its thinking. Deep-breathing hate-pleasure of expressing ourselves clearly. Too many words. Too many complexities that shouldn't be expressed for fear of treasoning our real feelings. A couple walking, separate but equal, equally edging the fences of the city's coupled woods where the wind is hiding. Each half of the couple containing newborn ideas hiding. Ideas of hate as explanation waiting to be thought. The couple walks in rhythm. Their internal monologue becomes a dialogue. They agree and let the other finish. Across the roofs of an entire capital, their knuckles bump repeatedly and both apologize. Giggle, and apologize, and try to remain hateful. But both begin to argue in the other's golden-scented best interest. Their own interest. They stop. Not their own interest, they remind themselves privately. They start again. They do it all over. It's torture, the earnest considerations of hate and the failings to perform. It's horror, the waiting to say things we do not mean. Things we have to say regardless. The couple, having placed an entire city between themselves in hopes of misunderstanding, makes plans to talk tomorrow. To really talk. To start with real speaking knowing full well they will say more confusing truths. Things they do not mean. Things they've perfectly understood already. The jaw-clenching hate of pleasure made by really and truly smiling.

There's something different about you.

What do you mean?

Something about you is different.

Is that a good thing?

It could be.

Could you be more descriptive?

I'm not sure I can. It's something familiar. Something I always struggled to understand about you.

But it's better now?

It might be.

Profound.

You'd be more interesting if you realized you weren't that interesting.

What is that supposed to mean?

That you're not that interesting.

Yeah? Says who?

Says me. And I should know.

Great. Very nice talking to you.

You're not listening to me.

Yes I am.

Well then you're not hearing me.

Maybe you're just not speaking loud enough.

Do you need me to scream it?

Maybe that's where we got things wrong.

Did you ever realize how much I liked you?

But did you ever love me?

See, you're not hearing me.

I must be too dull to understand.

No, you'd understand if you were duller.

Right.

At least smile. Doesn't it feel good to flirt?

Is that what we're doing?.

What is it you say, who's buried Grant's womb?

Tomb.

The breeze sets down in a trickling fountain, bathing its pleasure. Preening it. The high expands in the cold of water. The high, for a moment, thinks it's liquid. The roundabout's eyes dilate. Its muscles tighten. Its heartbeat taps its many toes. We take another to be safe, to safely maintain the storm. The moon tugs, beckons us as a referee does, away from the chaos. The fountain at the center of Place de La Réunion ripples, tries hard for its right to remain silent, to hold still. But the moon and the wind force motion fast upon it. The forces elicit the fountain's reaction. Without the fountain's permission. The stone pines of the Place come to life, and to the fountain's aid. Strong, sturdy, encircling, like our friend's friends we do not know. A couple of friends, same exactly as a couple in romance, enter the Place like a square, treat the Place like a boxing ring, though the square is circular. Obviously. The friends argue. They fight. The guilty pleasure of knowing we are completely right, inextricable from the sick sensing that, at the same time, we are entirely wrong. A guilty pleasure. The friends speak in phrases without objects, in a language unlearnable to the world. Unknowing cuts.

Unspeakable slights. And yet we glimpse the irreconcilable chance at retribution. Only the friendship knows how so. Not even the friends the chance concerns can see it now. Because friendship becomes the friend itself. An extra body in combat. One who says, *You're both being stupid.* The couple each say, *How could you. I didn't. You did. That isn't what I meant.* Each feels ridiculous, from the sound of the friendship laughing. They each bear down, scream, *fine,* knowing that it isn't. Knowing that it always will be. The guilt of pleasure in getting one over on a competitor when we know well and good there is hardly any prize.

If I have a kid, I want you to be the godfather.

Really?

Of course.

What does that entail?

I have no idea.

Does Jude's and Léa's baby have a godfather?

Yeah, me.

Really?

Yeah. Not that I treat him that godly, let alone fatherly.

Can you be godfather to more than one kid?

I don't think there are any rules against it.

So would you be my baby's godfather?

You don't want to interview me first?

Brilliant idea. Where do you see yourself in five years?

Godfather to two beautiful children.

Love the confidence. And how will you provide for my child, in the event of my untimely yet romantic demise?

You haven't heard? I'm rich.

Oh no, I've heard. Everyone's heard.

My reputation precedes me.

Confidence, check. Richness, check. And how will you teach my child the ways of the world?

The belt?

Not funny.

A little funny.

Only because we're high.

The streetlights are on, the moonlight is out, and the chemicals are ripping us open. Our winds of pleasure, breezy, like the children we will be. Children who must return home eventually. And so we go home, to Ménilmontant and to Belleville Park, with its platform overlooking the city. Every pleasure there you could possibly imagine, in cumulation. Our pleasure here, shaped as hills, constantly exploding with lindens. The linden trees have grown tall enough to partially obstruct our view. That park's access road, this pleasure's fast lane, Rue des Envierges, like a love tunnel, emptying us backward, returning the roundabout to itself, a black-lit traffic circle we know better than our lives. Our life. Its love. The breaks. We are only weights and fantasies. We are only heavy pride, heavy hate, heavy guilt, and terrible fear. And then we are a feathery yearning. With chemicals, we give in too quickly, to the fantasies, the rushes we were bound to bow down to eventually. Inevitably. Predeterminably. Weight slips away. The speed of our age gets chilling. Thins us. The preempted arrival of our futures feels great. The cold wind creates a sniffling. Voices carry on it. Our own voices. Memories and future tellings. Our sniffing mixes with the huffing of how we cope. The pleasure wind gets in, smelling of roundabout, finding our pleasure's source. A snow must be coming, for the kids are shifting, and though we sometimes shift in punishment, we mostly shift from coming weather.

More? One last one?

Definitely.

What time do you have the babysitter until?

Don't worry. He's with Léa's mom.

Amazing.

A whole one then?

Split it?

Perfect.

Do you want one too?

Yeah. Of course.

Ah, a whole one then. Come on.

Are there enough?

More than enough.

Go on.

That's more like it.

There's no way we're sleeping tonight.

Isn't that the point?

I guess it is.

We're all going back to Jude's and Léa's, yeah?

Yeah, we've already blown up the mattresses.

The mattresses be damned.

No Shakespeare shit tonight.

No drama kids this time.

Rachel will sing with me.
Where are Matt and Marie?
Outside, no?
I just came from outside.
Is Nathan outside?
Yeah, with Pierre.
But not Matt and Marie?
I didn't see them.

Back up. Or down, depending. The ups and downs of love. Our love, caught in the wind, caught up in itself. The histories of our loves past are all the same, same as all our future lovers, all the weathers, every precedented event felt as something new. Something uncanny. Every snowstorm, every winter, the same as every heatwave. Sometimes we hurt the people we love with how much love we have for them. Only sometimes do we remember the bad a person's love has done to us, and what punishments our love has done them back. Mainly, when we remember, we remember the lying down together, in the snow, trying to make an angel. In time, upon reflection, each and every love gets better. Because it is love. Every old story becomes new, and so, then, forgotten. Our better memories grow dangerous potential, our bad memories get covered in comfortable moss. But God, the drugs are good. Drugs so good that we re-narrate. Only now, from the inside out. A cycle of folding in on ourselves. We find dark and damp and private places, sheltered from the wind and the weather in it. We catch its pleasure in a trap. We free ourselves to reenact the past and thus begin regrowing.

Are we the extras?

What do you mean?

Are we the plus ones?

What makes you say that?

Sometimes I feel like we're the only two who see things coming.

I didn't see this coming. Did you?

From miles away.

What's that in kilometers?

Shut up.

Do you really feel like we're different?

Sometimes.

I guess you're right.

I feel bad for them.

For who?

What?

Who do you feel bad for?

Shit, I don't know anymore.

My point exactly. If they're happy, can't we just leave them alone?

How long do you think it will last this time?

Forever.

Really?

I promise.

I love you. Have I told you that already?

At least two hundred times this evening.

I do feel bad for him though. Don't you?

Who?

What do you mean who?

Him? Fuck him. He's not even an extra.

A worn-out roundabout, coming down, desperate, making silence. Behind our bar we find a wet-black back alley hiding. There are no toilets in it. No brooms. No cause for population. In the alley, all alone, are only two familiar people standing. In limited space. With limited time. Within selective memory. We are all the entire history of two people. We are used to forcing ourselves tight within our limits. We wait for nothing. We want for everything. We try, for a moment, to wake our guilt, our hate, our fear, our pride. We can't get them up. We go to ground. The cold wet ground of love. Our memories remember one another fondly. Green memories like the soft trees destined to outlive us. The time in the movie theater, surrounded by pulsing scenes. The first time, in the living room, surrounded by sleeping family. The best time, in the small park, surrounded by the trees. Matt and Marie, like all of us giving over to our truth. Giving up. Giving in. Caving to our pleasured airs. They know the bads and breaks of their action. They feel the we of their example. We feel the glory of our failures. How easy it is to only right our wrongs.

So then you, me, sweet drugs, old high, what do lovers make us? Rachel is right to feel jealous, toward a thing she doesn't want. This is the love psychosis, the love mathematic, the fear of passing chance. Pierre and Sarah are right to feel jealous, in their comparisons of passion. When love transcends the body, it can so easily obsess on lust. Eli is right to be a critic, wanting love in cleaner forms. Mess is so much faster made than any sort of magic. Jude and Léa are right to protect a belief that they are not the only ones. Love is a lonely justice. It frets at finding itself alone.

Have you guys seen Marie?

Wasn't she with you?

Clearly not.

Weird.

I haven't seen her for twenty minutes.

Sorry, Nathan.

For what?

Nothing. For nothing.

Is Matt gone too?

No idea.

Are you still high?

No.

Do you feel like another?

I don't think so.

Tu te casses?

Je crois, oui.

Get home safe.

Nathan walked off, or rather, drained away down Rue des Couronnes. Rachel, Jude, Léa, Eli, Pierre, and Sarah watched him go. Soon after, they were joined by Matt and Marie, who didn't ask where he'd gone. The circle stared at the quiet roundabout and pondered. Bracing. And rightly so. A wind now from the left, from the west. Rightly so that it should be the wind that lets us gently down. And so it was. Wind, with its divisions, icy gusts of individuality.

The wind became again what it has always been. What it is. A sensation. The cold, simply. The chemicals of our pleasure done diffusing. True cold hugged their bodies, sending them shifting, unlike the climax it sent before. The circle prepared in their lonely ways to face the comedown. A downshift to the drug night was always sure to come. But the bodies were together, bumping and rattling, wide-eyed at their closeness. A closeness that had forgotten faces, drugs that had forgotten their purpose, a night that passed without recognition. But one that the circle will remember later and have no idea why.

And then, with the night at its quietest, its most memorable, a stranger appeared out of the deep dark of Rue des Cascades like bleakness was his queue, sprinting wild and checking over his shoulder as he entered the roundabout. At the dead center of the circumscribed circle, he tripped and splayed. And so then appeared three shadowy figures, clearly in pursuit, who were, the three, triplets in the dark. They set upon the stranger, who from his splaying had made himself fetal. None of the eight friends spoke and neither did the roundabout. The three men, like boys with their ball, began to kick at the stranger's head. The kicks grew harder, as if they were trying to kick it in, as if they were trying to ruin their plaything. And harder. Harder. Nothing stopping them. Nothing getting in the way. Nothing intervening. No one so stupid as to get involved.

It was hard on us, when the aloneness started going round. It felt like everyone but us was changing. Until the change got to us too. Everyone we knew talked about authority. The authorities who came on good authority. They promised. They double promised. They told us not to go toward the screaming or the crying. They said it was healthy to worry, about one another, about what we were capable of doing. But we looked around, intrigued. We witnessed. All we could see was smiling, and it was chilling. We couldn't help but notice so many people helping. Shame on them. We couldn't stop ourselves admitting to seeing people giving up their precious food. To seeing people carrying those bags of food for those who couldn't lift them. We recognized the criminals, the grumpy who normally bumped one another, now happy to make room for bodies lifting bags. It was uplifting, the flouting of our authorities' recommended worry. Our hands went raw from repetitive washing, for the sake of flouting, to wash our hands of worry. For the sake of returning to community. We all noticed our hands rotting a little, from the helping, and then we all commented on noticing. After a month, our authorities got to saying nothing would be the same. To accept that. To accept it doubly. No matter how much we'd noticed, we couldn't stop ourselves from wondering. They told us it was really time to stop the helping now, or else. That it was us, or else. That really got to some of us. But not us. One of our friends got the most afraid and listened harder. She went out for the aloneness, to places with fewer and fewer people. She didn't help, because she was good. She was promised. People screamed and she walked on by, like a blessing. On one of her walks she was stopped by police. The cop said she was being unsafe, the cheek, and demanded her address. Then he demanded her number. He promised these were normal questions. They were for her safety. The cop said for her to message him the moment she got home safely. It was for her safety. His voice was full of echo. It seemed to make sense in the context. Our friend told herself to feel safe about it. That normal worries had died away. Our friend did what she was told. An hour passed and the cop messaged, could he come over later. To check on her safety. He knew where she lived, she didn't even have to tell him. The cop knew it for her safety. He reminded her of that. She messaged us, begging we come to protect her. But she was far away. Far enough that it was illegal now, to go. Remember, it was unsafe to help. And there were fleets of cops between us. They'd set up barriers. They called them barricades. But only the cops called them that. We didn't know what to do. We kept telling ourselves that we didn't know what to do. We kept telling ourselves that everyone was acting so friendly. The authorities kept telling us that nothing would be the same. Only, in the end, we kept learning that nothing was ever different.

Pierre and Sarah, as if they'd never left

What are you thinking?
　Nothing.
　Stop. What are you thinking?
　Nothing.
　Don't do that.
　Don't do what?
　You know what you're doing. What are you thinking?
　Nothing. Really.
　Nothing?
　It's just that...
　What?
　Never mind.
　Come on.
　It's nothing.
　Are you sure?
　I'm sure. Want to take a walk?
　Sure. Sure you're alright?
　Yeah. I'm fine. It was nothing.
　There was rougher land beyond the garden's post-and-wire fencing, land Pierre and Sarah owned, though sometimes hunters walked across it. The title clearly said the land was theirs but it was unclear if Pierre and Sarah were allowed to touch it. So the land still looked unownable and that worried Sarah. And it worried Pierre just as much. Shrubs, bushes, ferns. All unkempt. But in

the spring, tiny flowers. Pierre and Sarah had walked the land for nearly two years, since they determined it was theirs and they walked it so as to claim it, their feet cutting paths like streets into the wilderness where nothing grew now except for weeds. These paths made their walking slightly easier, if fractionally less natural. And marginally less romantic. Pierre and Sarah could take lefts if they wanted, at the big tree. Or rights, sometimes. Or they could just keep going straight and if they did they couldn't miss it.

The land boasted trees, so many trees, whose names and species Pierre and Sarah could never remember. Sarah had put something on her phone to learn about the trees, but then Sarah chastised herself for looking at her phone while walking. As such, the phone stayed in her pocket and neither Pierre nor Sarah ever learned the names correctly. All the better. Some of the trees were tall. As tall as buildings. Those became high rises. Others were middling and they became midrises. That is what they called them. Pierre and Sarah cut their paths to pass in front like the trees were buildings on a road. They would lean back on their walks, sometimes, trying to see into the living rooms of the trees where light cut through the foliage like windows. But Sarah and Pierre could never see in because the windows in the trees were always just moonlights or setting sunbeams caught in the branches.

At the back end of their land was a portion of lakeshore. The lake was small enough that it didn't lap but sometimes it rippled from fish jumping or from someone throwing a rock in. When they'd first moved to the land, Pierre and Sarah would get naked at night and enter the lake and they would swim out into the water far enough that it became lake they didn't own. There they would touch and feel the big and small things of one another's bodies touching and back on the shore, which they did own, the water would both lap and ripple. But they didn't really do that sort of thing anymore. Only sometimes.

It was mid-spring, not warm enough to swim. Both Pierre and Sarah felt relieved by the cool temperature. At that exact moment Pierre and Sarah knew their friends would be drinking at their bar on the roundabout, a few simple turns and a forty-minute train ride away. Instead of walking down by the water, Pierre and Sarah stayed to the left at the big tree and went deeper into the woods where it was darker, where they knew there was a clearing. It was too dark to see, but Sarah knew exactly where she was going and Pierre followed, worryingly, though he too knew exactly where they were heading. In the clearing, they looked up at the black outlines of the trees against the lighter black background of the sky. There were stars in the patch of sky made by the clearing and Pierre pointed them out. He held his phone to the stars and said, *Ursa Major*. Pierre had pointed out the stars every night for two years and it felt like the stars were always *Ursa Major*. Sarah tried to hold her breath and keep it from sounding exasperated.

Isn't it just the Big Dipper?

No, it's more than that.

Sarah didn't know where to let out her air from. She let

it slowly from her nose.

What?

Nothing.

What?

This is called a *copse*, apparently.

What is?

This. A circle of trees.

Cool.

Pierre thought only briefly about the word *copse*, then let the thought pass to focus on what Sarah was thinking. Sarah tried to hold on to the word *copse* but struggled. They both got quiet and looked around for eyes. Eyes were there, watching, and Pierre and Sarah could see them watching, but the eyes were disappointing. The eyes were animalian. Some low, crouching in bushes. Other eyes up in the branches perched high on long necks. But they were just the eyes of meat to be eaten. Nothing to love or stroke. Pierre tried to wink at the eyes and though some closed and others opened, the eyes only held back staring. Sarah had learned not to look too long at the eyes. Instead, Sarah invented a new game. Sarah pretended the copse was the roundabout, wrapped around with buildings. She stood closer to Pierre then took his hand and swung it lightly. Pierre understood and he pretended everyone was watching from high up in the trees. Sarah pretended too and for a second the pretending felt amazing.

I've been thinking.

Clearly.

Sorry.

What about?

Do you think they would all come and live with us? Out here?

Who?

Everyone.

What do you mean?

If they could, do you think everyone would move out here?

I don't understand.

I was just thinking, if there was somehow the space, would they come?

We only have two bedrooms.

I don't mean in our house. I mean out here. We have all this.

In tents?

The trees sat still. Sarah felt like they were eavesdropping and so she spoke a little louder, grinning.

No, like, what if everyone had a little cabin? With a little bedroom and a living room. And everyone had their own toilet. And then, what if there was a main building that was communal, with a kitchen and a dining room and a big living room with lots of sofas? Like, what if we put an addition onto the house and made that the social space?

Where would we live?

I don't know. Maybe we'd have our own cabin. So it was equal.

I don't know.

We have all that money for the renovations. We could do it, technically.

You mean your mom's money?

Yeah.

You said you didn't want to touch that until we knew what we were doing.

What if this is what we were doing?

I don't know.

And if we get that money your dad is supposed to give you we'd have more than we knew what to do with.

Sarah, I told you, I really don't know if he'll give me any more.

Sorry. I was just thinking. I wasn't being serious.

The copse shifted uncomfortably in the wind. The wind licked at the young trees, which bent away from it, and in their bending they made the clearing a little smaller. Sarah tried not to think too seriously. Pierre felt bad for snapping.

Jude and Léa would probably love it, I guess. Maybe Matt too, if Jude moved. I'm not sure about Marie or Eli. And I know it wouldn't work for Rachel.

Sarah smiled and put both her arms around Pierre.

Come on, they would. They're always talking about coming out and staying for a while. They always say it would be like a little vacation.

Besides Léa, they've only ever come out here, what, twice?

Think how peaceful it would be, to have them all here. If everyone had their little space. We could be together sometimes. And alone. We have so much space that everyone could be pretty far apart.

It would be nice to see Jude.

Wouldn't it? And everyone's life would be so much less stressful, not having to deal with Paris all the time. It would be cheaper. Fewer people. Less pollution. And the lake.

Sarah winked at Pierre and Pierre smiled a little. Or at least he tried to.

It would make sense, since we're getting older.

We're not old.

We're almost thirty. Think how pragmatic it would be. We would split costs on everything, so life would be cheaper for everyone. And Matt and Eli could finally stabilize. We'd all have responsibilities, so we wouldn't have to do all the work, which Léa would love. And when people had kids, we could all help take care of them. And I know that would help Rachel. Think about it. It takes a village. One person could care for all the kids by themselves one day a week. And then we'd each have six days off to explore ourselves. And then the kids would understand adults differently. They'd learn love from other sources. It wouldn't be so nuclear. And we could make the garden bigger and grow food all year. We could almost turn it into a farm or something.

Being a farmer would be funny.

It would be safer too, to build our own community out here, with them. There wouldn't be so many people involved. We'd know exactly who was affecting us, so we'd be safe. Like how Jude and Léa are always talking about not trusting people they'd thought they trusted. And the air would be cleaner. And no metros. None of that stress anymore.

Jude and Léa can be a bit too much, about that. They've gone a bit paranoid.

I know. But I'm not sure we can really understand it though. I'm sure it would be more interesting to raise kids like that, where they had siblings but in a different way. In a new way. A new kind of family.

Kids?

It sounds nice in that way, doesn't it?

It does.

Sarah imagined herself wearing sturdy, calf-length boots and thick, white-fading blue jeans cuffed over the boots. In her picture, the button fly of her jeans was ticked open to allow for her belly, which had grown enormous. Sarah touched her real belly, the one she considered tight and perfect, and still winced at the idea. She pictured herself stomping through the trees, slightly clown-footed, with the sound of dirt and gravel stones crunching under the tread of the good boots. She knocked on the door to one of the cabins, smoke leaking out from a chimney pipe in the single pitched eave. The door opened and Sarah saw the future. The future was dressed in a plump, flowing dress made of recycled linen and printed over with a vegetal pattern, the pattern matching the land like a camouflage. Marie and Rachel were standing there, both enormous in the doorway inside the functional dresses, holding one another around the waists, and they were giggling. They were an advertisement. They invited her in. Inside, Marie and Rachel were at work butchering animals and tanning hides, or whatever American homesteaders knew to do in the videos she'd be secretly watching, turning them off when Pierre entered the room. Videos of blood off camera and natural material and tough women always giggling, unabashedly plumping.

You've never said anything like that before.

Yes I have.

You definitely haven't.

Don't talk about it.

I won't.

It's different if it doesn't isolate me.

I thought we weren't talking about it.

We're not.

Pierre worked himself up to imagining. His thoughts took him back to his lake and he imagined himself fishing, something he didn't know how to do. Pierre liked the clip and rattle the gear and tools made in the instructional videos he'd be watching. He liked when the men put the knots in their mouth just before the synching, to help with the friction, or so they said. Pierre giggled to himself but Sarah didn't hear him. With his imagination, Pierre imagined everything between himself and Jude had washed away. He said to Jude, *Look at the sky. Today's gonna be gooooood fishing.* The sky was kind of teal, and clouded over, and Pierre told Jude a joke he wouldn't have wanted Sarah to hear. The water rippled in laughter. It felt good to tell the joke and not to have repercussions. From his waders, Jude produced two cigars and called them *stogies.* Jude trimmed and lit Pierre's cigar and it felt good rolling the thick smoke around in his mouth. With one hand Pierre smoked and with the other he fished and it even felt better to throw a fishing rod into his imagination, the red and white ball on the line floating in the dreamy wake, and Pierre pulled back two fish on the same throw, or cast, or whatever you call it.

Think how nice dinners would be. We'd have a big wooden table. Like the ones that look like they're made out of trees. And it would be *laden*. And it would be big enough for all our families to sit around. And we'd have those plates made of raw fired clay.

All the food would be heaped on big platters, so it sort of felt like a feast every night, with huge piles of steaming food.

You mean a banquet.

Yes, a banquet!

Have you read *Look Homeward, Angel?*

You had me read it.

Well the food would be like that.

The dinners the group had now were usually at Jude's and Léa's and they were growing duller by the course. Their apartment was too small, even for Jude and Léa and the baby, and the group would sit crammed on mismatched furniture, plates on their laps, spilling food down their shirts. It wasn't a way to live. But the location wasn't what was driving the friends apart. It was the menu. Since Jude and Léa had had their kid, they'd become a couple who shopped exclusively at Biocoop and Bio c' Bon and Naturalia. They talked about being responsible with their food, for their kid, and for the world. They repeated themselves endlessly. They didn't allow meat in their house. If Matt brought any charcuterie, they wouldn't let him use their plates. If Rachel asked for something a bit more *gourmand*, the two would scoff and lecture. And the change was only accelerating. What had at first been well-sourced vegetarian had quickly turned vegan. When Jude and Léa got bored, they went deeper. Now, what they served was usually raw and not enough. There'd been the night of kale salad with quinoa and no dressing. That dinner had become privately infamous among the other six. And there'd been the night with seitan marinated in nut milk with no salt added or offered. Sarah, Pierre, and the rest of the group would leave the dinners tense. The only things keeping the dinners going were Léa's and Jude's insistence and the new tradition of the six going to a kebab shop to fill up on a second dinner immediately after.

Think how much more we could afford with everyone pitching in. Like nice kitchen stuff. Like a KitchenAid.

And good knives.

And a van we could all fit in and go camping. One of those vans with a kitchen in them.

A van?

Yeah. It's something Marie and Rachel and I have always talked about.

Always?

Since we met. We'd have tents set up around a cool old van, and we would have coffee and everyone would be all sleepy and lazy in their big wooly jumpers. And then we'd go on a hike and come back relaxed and sit around a fire.

Very specific.

Not bad though, no?

No, it sounds lovely.

If everyone gets a real job in the next few years, it would be crazy. We could do so much. Everyone would have to put a portion of their salary toward the group.

The group had gone on vacation together twice a year for the last three years. It was not an uncommon thought among them to wonder if they would make it a fourth year. Pierre and Sarah always paid the up-front costs, the house, the liquor, the week of groceries. The two of them liked arriving at the house early, before everyone, filling the fridge with everything possible, laying out the cases of wine and beer on the floor next to the fridge, and then appreciating the need to consume, or else waste. Like it was a challenge. The group consumed, and some cleaned up, and some lay by the pool, and they went to bed at drastically different times, and they did the same things over and over for a week. When the weeks were finished, Sarah would total up the costs, split them evenly using an app on her phone and then ask everyone to transfer their share to her bank. Two years earlier, during the summer holiday, Matt had been out of a job but had still decided to come. He'd had fun, it was obvious, and the group had been happy for him since it felt like he'd achieved some distraction. He'd eaten and drank like the rest of them, too much, and to the point of getting drunk. But at the end of the week, when Sarah sent out the expenses, Matt claimed he'd eaten and drank less than the others. On purpose. To save. That he hadn't had the meat or the champagne or the good cheeses. Marie reminded Matt that he had. She'd watched him. But Matt ignored her and said he should owe less. It became awkward in the weeks that followed and privately some of the others said it had ruined their relaxation. But eventually they said, *Matt doesn't have a job, and he was so happy, so...*and the group had agreed and covered some of his costs. But five months later, during the winter holiday in the snow, when Matt was working and making good money, he pulled the trick again, refusing his even share of the balance. He said he'd brought his own wine, since he didn't like *the natural piss* they were drinking, so he shouldn't have to pay for the liquor kitty. Marie reminded him that he had chugged the boxed wine from the plastic faucet. He responded that was one time, as a gag. But it wasn't one time. When they returned to Paris, with a rare snow falling, seven of them met at a bar they never went to. Matt was not invited, but still they argued. They were mad. Eli claimed he hadn't had the fish. Pierre said he hadn't eaten the fruit. Eli even suggested that Matt not be invited next year, so he'd learn. *A lesson*, Marie said. But as the night went on and they overtalked the issue the mad relented. No one was willing to be the one to tell Matt he was uninvited. Drunk, the seven split Matt's unpaid share and worked his future costs into their budget.

We would split up the responsibilities. Everyone would have their little skill that they contributed.

Like what?

I don't know. You're pretty good at building stuff. You could build things for the farm. Chicken coops, or things like that.

What would you do?

Gardening, I guess. Maybe.

Rachel had that phase where she was making clothes and learning to knit, didn't she?

Yeah, exactly. And Marie is good with kids, so she could be the teacher.

Are we becoming homeschoolers now?

No. The kids would go to school. Marie would be the nanny then.

Jude has started doing some investing, on the side.

Has he?

Yeah. And Léa works in production. She could manage the overall planning and schedules and whatever.

It would be sort of like a commune. Matt's always going on about that sort of thing.

What would Eli do?

What *would* Eli do?

I don't know, chop wood?

Eli? Chop wood?

He's got the beard for it.

Eli was becoming increasingly late to everything, well beyond the accepted fifteen minutes. He was constantly showing up in the middle or the end of get-togethers, flopping down on a chair or couch, not even apologizing. Or if he was on time, he would have to leave early. Eli would complain that he was tired. That he hadn't slept, and then he would take over the conversation with his complaints like he was trying to get sympathy. At first, the group discussed the issue. It wasn't like Eli's job was all that difficult. His tutoring let him set his own hours. What confused the group, what hurt them, was how Eli never made it clear where he'd been or where he was going. More importantly, he never said who with. Sometimes he said he had *a meeting*. Other times he had *family dinners*. But the meetings and dinners were becoming more frequent and the group was bucked against the developing truth that Eli couldn't be relied on. Sometimes, in being unwilling to accept it, the group found themselves hurt. Most recently, on Jude's birthday, Léa had given Eli the keys to their apartment so the group could prepare a surprise dinner party. Léa was going to meet Jude after work, distract him for a while with a drink at the bar and tell him that all his friends were busy that night, sorry. The group had shown up to the apartment on time, like they were supposed to. Everyone except Eli. They waited in the building courtyard, in the cold, as their prep time shrank. They called Eli and he didn't answer. They called again. And when they heard the door to the courtyard open, they thought it was finally him. But it wasn't. It was Jude and Léa and their kid. And Jude looked surprised, but not in a good way. Léa looked sad. And the kid laughed and giggled like he normally did, without knowing. Jude said, *Sorry guys, I have an early morning at work tomorrow, so I've got to get to bed soon.* The seven of them climbed up to the tiny apartment and they had a quiet drink together, barely even taking off their coats, barely even turning on music. And then right as they were getting ready to leave, Eli opened the door acting like he was right on time. He even used the key Léa had given him.

And you're always talking about being worried that we're both only children and that...

You're worried too.

I am, yeah. And this would be a way to have a bigger family. It would be like getting free aunts and uncles.

For our kids?

Yeah, and siblings for us.

Sure.

And then we'd be connected to everyone else's family.

Like Matt's dad.

Matt's dad! Jesus, he's nice, isn't he?

And Léa's parents.

Also great. And Rachel's parents.

Rachel's parents?

What?

Really?

Shit. Obviously. Sorry.

Don't worry about it. They are rich.

That helps.

Do you think your parents would get on board?

They've always wanted lots of grandchildren.

Grandchildren who look like them.

Not necessarily. They've gone soft in their old age. What about your parents?

Hard to say.

Your mom keeps sending me videos of children I've never even heard of. I'm sure she'd be into it.

That would be nice, having her around more.

What about Marie? Definitely not her parents?

I'm not sure Marie would be willing to live around children.

Her anti-procreation bent is just a front, don't you think?

Maybe. Would you let her sisters live with us?

Are they still living with her?

Sometimes.

Well then of course.

We're quickly becoming a cult.

You would love that.

There'd been a time, when everyone first met, that Marie still lived at home with her parents, back when Marie and Matt were first dating and Jude and Pierre lived together next to Belleville Park and Sarah had inherited the sprawling apartment in the Sixth from her dead grandmother. Sarah, and not Pierre, had been the first to notice the change in Marie. Her lagging. Her attempts to stay out later. Her constantly checking in with her sisters. At first, it felt like a turnoff, for Sarah, that Pierre seemed only to be friends with broken women. For a while Sarah was afraid it indicated something about herself. That Pierre would love her. But so goes the paranoia of budding love. And because Sarah was new to the group, she felt well placed to be objective. After a long night when Marie repeatedly crossed the street to scream into her phone, and without asking Pierre, Sarah pulled Marie aside and proposed that Marie and her sisters come live with her. She had plenty of space. Her dead grandmother would have loved the apartment having more life, which was a lie. Without a moment's hesitation, Marie accepted, as if she'd expected such a salvation, not necessarily from Sarah, but maybe from God. When Sarah told Pierre what she'd done, she worried he'd find it too presumptive, too serious a step for the two of them. Instead he seemed to fall deeper in love, faster even than Marie had accepted the offer. For a while the situation was nice, having roommates who contributed new energy, who put on old songs from Sarah's childhood, who cooked terrible new recipes from the internet, and who made Sarah feel better about her excesses. But it didn't last. Marie's parents found out where their children were living. And they showed up. At the door, or outside the windows yelling in their slurred French. They weren't like Rachel's parents, who performed their tortures in private. Marie's parents said terrible things to Marie so the entire world could hear it. The words flew down the stairs of the building and into neighbors' entryways, out the windows of the building and into neighbors' living rooms. The neighbors returned the screaming to Sarah, and to Pierre who was sleeping over more often. And then they filed formal complaints, both the neighbors and Marie's parents. Sarah and Pierre told the neighbors it was only temporary, even though they wanted Marie and her sisters to stay. But Marie heard them shushing the neighbors at the door and told them it was probably time she found somewhere else for them to go. She did. The big apartment then felt eerie, with only Sarah and Pierre in it, so Sarah sold it. Marie couldn't find a way to support her sisters, so eventually they ended up back at Marie's parents'. And in recent months, as Marie and Matt started talking about never having a family, Pierre and Sarah had begun to notice traces of her parents' violence in the tone of Marie's dialogue.

But I think the best part about it would be the good conversations all the time.

Mmm.

If we had everyone around, we'd have more people to have good conversations with, and then our conversations would be nicer too. They'd become even more interesting.

Don't worry. I understand.

Sorry, I didn't mean it like that.

No. I agree.

How nice it would be to have little debates every night. Like we have at the bar. That sort of knowledge sharing would be really special. I feel like it more than anything would improve everyone's quality of life. It's like life-long learning.

And I guess new people would be around a lot. Like boyfriends and girlfriends, or whatever. There would often be fresh energy.

Yeah, until people settled down with a partner.

If.

Rachel was dating a new boy who wasn't much different from any of the old boys she'd dated already. He looked like a washed-up member of The Libertines, or worse, BB Brunes, with messy hair that grew long at the temples and filled in for sideburns he still couldn't grow. His hair so much of his personality. Same as every one of Rachel's boyfriends. Though maybe this one was worse, in a way that Rachel or the rest of the circle couldn't see, the progressive worseness of each boyfriend setting the standard a little lower, men who said and did things to Rachel only slightly more shocking than the last. More simply, his name was not Maxime, though maybe it should have been. Maybe that would have been preferable. Whatever his name was, he reminded Rachel of the same person. Maybe her father, maybe her first, maybe a total stranger, but a person she would never admit to. Possibly because she hadn't figured the answer out herself. Nonetheless, this new boy spoke over her. He laughed at her points but not at her jokes. He thought he dominated her, which Rachel observed, contemplated, and allowed him to go on thinking. This new boy talked about her male friends a lot, when they were alone. And he tried to subjugate the other boys in the group, intellectually, whenever they were all together. He'd say, *Come on*, and, *You can't honestly believe that*. Matt would scoff and flex at these sentences. Jude and Pierre would just get quiet. Rachel's boyfriend didn't try to dominate the other girls, and there was just as much to be said in that. A lot that had been said, again and again, by the group and the world already. Only when he'd been so abrasive that the group was stunned into silence did he then get cute, or nice enough. And he could be very cute and nice enough when he wanted, which was the worst part about him. Rachel used those moments against the group, saying that he was cute and nice most of the time, and that the group just didn't see everything. But the group did see. They'd grown dull to the repetition. Repetition of character. The sort of repetition of self-surrounding that makes the emotionally interested miss the truth as a form of self-protection and self-avoidance. Or maybe self-flagellation. The sort of repetition and self-destruction that makes the days go faster and feel shorter, hoping for a new day, the next day, with something new in it, someone better in it, a subconsciously better self, until the next days merge to make a pattern. The pattern making a life.

If we had a kid, would we speak to it in French or English? Both, no?

Would you do one and I do the other?

How would we speak to each other?

I had a friend who grew up hating her father because he spoke English.

Well you can be the English speaker then.

Do you think they would actually do it?

All of them? I don't know. Maybe.

It isn't like we're that far from Paris. The train's only forty minutes. It's perfect really, to be removed but not fully disconnected.

That's why we moved here, isn't it?

In the copse, not unlike the roundabout, Pierre's and Sarah's imaginations were set against time and the time made everything real. Time drew their friends' faces from

the roundabout to the forest, their lives to the countryside. The reality made wrinkles. Faces in time took on
crow's-feet and laugh lines. Their faces became majestic.
Portraiture at first. Then five years and twenty years and
fifty of turning, morphing the faces into stone-honored
busts. In the time, cabins went up. And so did additions.
The faces went grayer and the cabins went browner.
Lovers were taken up, and babies were made and put out
to playing. New paths were cut by feet into nature. The
paths became streets and earned traffic. Commotions
were made toward the growing and the chopping and the
knitting. Fish were caught, vacuum-sealed, and distributed.
Cakes got baked and portioned and games got won and
done over. Knowledge was spread beyond heirs. There
was fairness in the rewards and the punishment. There
was fairness in the further additions. Neighborhoods were
born and known for their uniqueness. Hiding places were
found and given legend. Dinners were cooked and set on
platters. Salt and pepper were passed around and thanked
for politely. Storms came and leaks were created and hands
came together to plug the holes. There were dances. There
were stagings. There became unspoken codes of conduct.
There was laughter heard, and feet that ran to it. There
were nicknames lost and found. There became places of
honor. And trees around which celebrations congregated.
Knickknacks were nailed to trees that became memorials.
Memorials were visited on determined days. Hot summers
emptied glass cupboards and set the glasses to clinking.
Cold winters emptied mug cupboards that promised

them steam. Time became a government of gestures to manage the turning and its changing. Time was unanimously elected mayor.

You're very broody today.

Or am I just brooding?

How Danish of you.

I've told you, no more Shakespeare references.

But thoughts of the city infected the countryside, with its glory but also with its failure. Each day reduced the quality of escape. Each day brought the inescapable arguments of progress. Of time, and its corruption. And of maybes. The way maybes turn around on themselves and can go on turning if one is not careful. Maybe Marie became her family, incapable of stopping herself from yelling down on those around her. Maybe Matt couldn't pay for his presence and felt entitled to that distinction. Maybe Jude and Léa became jaded by their rightness. Maybe Rachel found another partner who everyone hated even better. Maybe Eli got fed up with expectations. Maybe the city became unequal, and violent, like they tend to. Maybe some streets in nature became safer than others. Maybe those issues were accepted, like they often are, because time and its poverty force acceptance. And maybe, in time, those maybes got faster. Dizzying. Maybe Marie's violence turned physical. Maybe Matt slept with Rachel, though he lived in a cabin with Marie. Maybe Jude and Léa stopped coming to dinner and taught their kid not to trust. Maybe Eli stayed up too late, too many times, and turned into a woodland hermit. Maybe, in the end, Pierre and Sarah felt stifled a second time and decided to move farther away. The maybes of time were terrifying. They spun up a ghost town in and of themselves. But maybe the roundabout bucked its nature and stopped turning. And so nature returned, looked around, and continued. The circle growing mosses and ivy. The growth covering corners and boring new holes. Like the roundabout, maybe nature reclaimed space until it found its beginning, until it turned back on itself and ended where it began. The traffic circle becoming a copse. The copse Pierre and Sarah were stuck in.

Pierre looked at Sarah and saw the privilege he'd never criticized. Her freedom to think utopic. He saw the funding, which allowed her to think ridiculously. He loved it, but maybe he could hate her for it. Maybe, in time. Maybe one day, when he was old, he would wake to find her building something beautifully unsustainable for them, the good life they'd dreamed up, that she'd pushed him to achieve, and hate her more for her success.

Sarah looked at Pierre and saw the failings she'd never questioned. The chance he'd taken to live his zen. She perceived the risk he'd taken to find the average pointless. She loved it, and maybe it would ruin him for her. Maybe one day, when she was old, his relaxation she'd always wanted to adopt would reveal itself an atrophy. Maybe she'd learn the love she felt for him was just as useless as everything else.

Pierre and Sarah looked at one another, got angry, and wondered what the other was thinking. They each tried to start a sentence and failed. Rachel, Matt, Jude, Léa, Marie, and Eli left the bar and stepped into the roundabout. They were far away, but close enough. They could sense the fighting coming, and asked Pierre and Sarah to wait until tomorrow.

Can we put a pause on this discussion?

I was just about to ask you the same thing.

Sarah and Pierre looked up at the circle space of sky made by the copse. They listened. They agreed. They breathed in the air of warm spring turning to summer. The lakeshore was too far from where they stood. First Sarah took off her clothes and when she was naked, so did Pierre. They both giggled. Their bodies were young again, tight in the cold, hard in the present. They were alone and distracted from it by being so. They looked at one another without touching. They giggled more. They lay down on their damp patch of nature. They spread their arms and felt the wet against their backs. The wet felt good. The cold from the wet felt refreshing. They looked at one another and smiled.

What are you thinking?

It would never work, would it?

No, I don't think it would.

It might though, no? Maybe?

It would be cool if it could.

ACKNOWLEDGEMENTS

I would like to thank my publisher, Dallas Hudgens, and my editor, Jules Hucke.